Death *of a* Valentine

Previous Hamish Macbeth Mysteries by M. C. Beaton

M.C. BEATON

Death *of a* Valentine

GRAND CENTRAL
PUBLISHING

NEW YORK   BOSTON

Grand Central Publishing
Hachette Book Group
237 Park Avenue
New York, NY 10017

www.HachetteBookGroup.com

Printed in the United States of America

First Edition: January 2010
10 9 8 7 6 5 4 3 2 1

Grand Central Publishing is a division of Hachette Book Group, Inc.
The Grand Central Publishing name and logo is a trademark of Hachette Book Group, Inc.

Library of Congress Cataloging-in-Publication Data

Beaton, M. C.
    Death of a valentine / M.C. Beaton.
      p. cm.
    ISBN 978-0-446-54738-3
    1. MacBeth, Hamish (Fictitious character)—Fiction. 2. Police—Scotland—Highlands—Fiction.
    3. Policewomen—Scotland—Highlands—Fiction. 4. Highlands (Scotland)—Fiction. I. Title.
    PR6053.H4535D347 2010
    823'.914—dc22
                                                                      2009006083

For my husband, Harry Scott Gibbons.
And my agent, Barbara Lowenstein.
With love.

To Minerva

My temples throb, my pulses boil,
I'm sick of Song and Ode and Ballad—
So, Thyrisis, take the Midnight Oil
And pour it on a lobster salad.

My brain is dull, my sight is foul,
I cannot write a verse or read—
Then, Pallas, take away thine Owl,
And let us have a lark instead.

—Thomas Hood

Death *of a* Valentine

Prologue

Over the heathery flanks of the mountains, over the lochs, over the vast tracts of land that make up the county of Sutherland in the very north of Scotland, down to the fishing boats bobbing at anchor along the west coast, the amazing news spread.

That most famous of highland bachelors, Police Sergeant Hamish Macbeth, was to be married at last. No, nothing like that mistake he had made before when he had nearly married some Russian. This was love. And he was to be married, right and proper, with a white wedding in the church in his home village of Lochdubh.

He was to marry his constable, Josie McSween, who had helped him solve the Valentine's Day murder. Pretty little thing she was, with glossy brown hair and big brown eyes. The whole village of Lochdubh adored Josie. And everyone could see she was in love with Hamish.

On the great day, the church was full to bursting. Some wondered if the former love of Hamish's life, Priscilla Halburton-Smythe, would attend, but others whispered she was in Australia.

The added excitement was that Elspeth Grant, former reporter and now a star television news presenter, had promised to attend. She had many fans, and some had brought along their autograph books.

Josie's father was dead and she appeared not to have any male relatives. She was to be given away by Police Superintendent Peter Daviot.

There was a rustle of excitement as the bride arrived. Hamish stood erect at the altar, flanked by his best man, Detective Sergeant Jimmy Anderson. "Cheer up!" muttered Jimmy. "Man, you're as white as a sheet."

The service began. Then at one point, the minister, Mr. Wellington, addressed the congregation. "If any amongst you know of any reason why this man and this woman should not be joined in holy matrimony, speak now, or forever hold your peace." His deep highland voice held a note of amusement. For who could protest such a love match?

Hamish Macbeth raised his eyes to the old beams of the church roof and murmured desperately the soldier's prayer.

"Dear God, if there is a God, get me out of this!"

Chapter One

It's hardly in a body's pow'r.
Tae keep, at times, frae being sour.

—Robert Burns

A year earlier

Hamish Macbeth had been promoted to sergeant. Having been promoted before and then reduced to the ranks, he had not even had to sit the necessary exams. Many a constable would have welcomed the promotion and the extra money that came with it, but Hamish was dismayed for two reasons. He was not an ambitious man and saw every rise up the ranks as a move to get him transferred to the city of Strathbane. All he wanted was to be left peacefully alone in his village police station.

He was also dismayed by being told that a constable would be coming to work with him and to clear out his spare room. The spare room was very highland in that it was stuffed with all sorts of rusting odds and ends that Hamish had picked up from time to time and had stored in the happy thought that they might come in useful one day.

At first he was confident that no one would want the job, but then he was told to expect a police constable, McSween.

He received a visit from his friend Detective Sergeant Jimmy Anderson. Jimmy walked in without knocking and found Hamish gloomily studying the contents of the spare room.

"For heaven's sakes, man," exclaimed Jimmy. "Get a move on. The lassie'll be here any minute."

Hamish Macbeth, all six feet and five inches of him, turned slowly round. "What lassie?"

"Your new copper. Wee Josie McSween."

Hamish's hazel eyes looked blank with shock. "Nobody told me it was a woman."

"I overheard that curse o' your life, Blair, telling Daviot that the influence of a good woman was just what you need."

Detective Chief Inspector Blair loathed Hamish and was always looking for ways to upset him.

"Come into the kitchen," said Hamish. "She cannae be staying here."

"Why not? Got any whisky?"

"Usual place. Help yourself. No, she'll need to find lodgings."

"It's the twenty-first century, Hamish. Nobody'll think anything of it."

Jimmy sat down at the kitchen table and poured himself a drink. He was a smaller man than Hamish, with sandy hair and blue eyes in a foxy face.

"The twenty-first century has not arrived in Lochdubh,"

said Hamish. "Chust you sit there and enjoy your drink. I've got calls to make."

Jimmy smiled and lay back in his chair. Although the month was April, a blizzard was blowing outside, "the lambing blizzard" as the crofters bitterly called it, that storm which always seemed to hit the Highlands just after the lambs were born. The woodstove glowed with heat. Hamish's dog, Lugs, snored in a corner and his wild cat, Sonsie, lay over Jimmy's feet. He could hear Hamish making urgent phone calls from the police office but could not hear what he was saying.

At last, Hamish came back into the kitchen, looking cheerful. "That's settled," he said. "All the women from the minister's wife down to the Currie sisters are phoning up headquarters to complain. Mrs. Wellington has a spare room at the manse, and that's where she's going."

"Josie's quite a tasty wee thing," said Jimmy. "What an old-fashioned dump this place is!"

"Better than that sink of a place, Strathbane," said Hamish. "It's snowing like hell. The road'll be blocked."

But in the fickle way of April blizzards, the snow abruptly stopped, the dark clouds rolled up the mountains, and soon a hot spring sun was rapidly melting the snow.

Josie set out, her heart beating with excitement. She was fairly small for a policewoman. She had masses of glossy brown hair and wide brown eyes. Her figure was a little on the plump side. Josie had fallen in love with the now legendary Hamish Macbeth some months before. She had read up on all the cases he had solved. The minute she had heard of the vacancy at Lochdubh, she had promptly applied. In the boot of her car, along with her luggage, was a carton of cookery books. Her mother who lived in Perth had always said that the way to a man's heart was through the kitchen door.

The sun shone down on the melting snow in the road in front of her. Mountains soared up to a newly washed blue sky. Perth, where Josie had been brought up, was just south of the highland line, and family visits had always been to the south—to Glasgow or Edinburgh. She found the whole idea of the Highlands romantic.

As her little Toyota cruised down into Lochdubh, she gave a gasp of delight. Whitewashed eighteenth-century cottages fronted the still waters of the sea loch. The pine forest on the other side of the loch was reflected in its waters. Melting snow sparkled in the sunlight.

The police station had an old-fashioned blue lamp hanging outside. Josie drew up and parked her car. She could already imagine herself cooking delicious meals for Hamish while he smiled at her fondly and said, "Whatever did I do without you?"

The front gate was difficult to open. She finally managed and went up the short path to the door and knocked loudly.

A muffled voice from the other side of the door reached her ears. "Go round to the side door."

Back out and round the side of the police station went Josie. Hamish Macbeth was standing by the open kitchen door looking down at her quizzically.

"I'm Josie McSween," said Josie. "I'll just get my things."

"You can't move in here," said Hamish. "The villagers won't

have it. You're to stay with Mrs. Wellington, the minister's wife."

"But—"

"There are no buts about it. The ladies of the village won't thole a lassie living with me at the police station. I'll get my coat and walk ye up there. When you see where it is, you can come back for your car. Wait there, McSween, I'll get my coat."

McSween! In all her dreams he had called her Josie. Hamish emerged shortly and began to walk off with long strides in the direction of the manse while Josie scurried behind him.

"Don't I get a choice of where I want to live?" she panted.

"You're a policewoman," said Hamish over his shoulder. "You just go where you're put."

The manse was situated behind the church. It was a Georgian building. Georgian architecture usually conjures a vision of elegance, but Scottish Georgian can be pretty functional and bleak. It was a square three-story sandstone building, unornamented, and with several windows bricked up dating from the days of the window tax.

Hamish led the way round to the kitchen door where Mrs. Wellington was already waiting, the highland bush telegraph having noticed and relayed every moment of Josie's arrival.

Josie's heart sank even lower. Mrs. Wellington was a vast tweedy woman with a booming voice.

"Where are your things?" she asked.

"I left them in my car at the police station," said Josie.

"Shouldn't you be in uniform?"

"It's my day off."

"Off you go, Mr. Macbeth," said Mrs. Wellington. "I'll just

show Miss McSween her room and give her the rules of the house and then she can bring her luggage."

Josie followed Mrs. Wellington into the manse kitchen. It was vast, dating from the days when ministers had servants and large families. It was stone-flagged, and the double sinks by the window were deep and made of stone with old-fashioned brass taps. A long dresser lining one wall contained blue and white plates. The newest item was a scarlet fuel-burning Raeburn stove. High up in the ceiling by a wooden pulley burned a dim single lightbulb. On the pulley hung a row of Mrs. Wellington's knickers: large, cotton, and fastened at the knee with elastic. Where on earth did one get knickers like that these days, wondered Josie. People didn't often talk about *knickers* any more, preferring the American *panties*. But *panties* suggested something naughty and feminine. In one corner stood a large fridge and, wonder of wonders in this antique place, a dishwasher.

"Come along," ordered Mrs. Wellington. "The washing machine is in the laundry room over there to your left. Washing is on Thursdays."

Josie followed her out of the kitchen, which led into a dark hall where a few dim, badly painted portraits of previous ministers stared down at her. There was a hallstand of the kind that looked like an altar and a Benares brass bowl full of dusty pampas grass.

The staircase was of stone, the steps worn smooth and polished by the long years of feet pounding up and down. At the first landing, Mrs. Wellington led the way along a corridor painted acid green on the top half, the bottom half being made of strips of brown-painted wood.

The wind had risen, and it moaned about the old manse like a banshee. Mrs. Wellington pushed open a door at the end. "This is where you'll stay. The arrangement is for bed and breakfast. Any other meals you want you will cook yourself, but not between five and six which is when I prepare tea for Mr. Wellington."

To Josie's relief the room was light and cheerful. The window looked out over the roofs of the waterfront houses to the loch. There was a large double bed with a splendid patchwork quilt covering it. A peat fire was burning in the hearth.

"We are fortunate to have a large supply of the peat so you can burn as much as you like," said Mrs. Wellington. "Now, once you are settled in, you will have your tea with us, seeing as it is your first day, and in the evening I will take you to a meeting of the Mothers' Union in the church hall to introduce you to the other ladies of Lochdubh."

"But Hamish——" began Josie weakly.

"I have told him of the arrangements and he has agreed. You are to report to the police station tomorrow morning at nine o'clock. When you drive up, you can leave your car outside the front door for easy access, but after that, use the kitchen door. Here are the keys. The only one you need to use is the kitchen door key."

The key was a large one, no doubt dating from when the manse had been built.

Josie thanked her and scurried off down the stairs. The mercurial weather had changed and a squall of sleet struck her in the face. She had been to the hairdresser only that morning. On her road back to the police station, the malicious wind whipped her hair this way and that, and gusts of icy sleet punched her in the face.

She knocked at the police station door but there was no answer. Josie got into her car and drove up to the manse.

She struggled up the stairs with two large suitcases. The manse was silent except for the moan of the wind.

In her room, there was a huge Victorian wardrobe straight out of Narnia. She hung away her clothes. Josie wanted a long hot bath. She walked along the corridor, nervously pushing open door after door until she found a large bathroom at the end. There was a claw-footed bath with a gas heater over it. The heater looked ancient but the metre down on the floor looked new. She crouched down and read the instructions. "Place a one-pound coin in the metre and turn the dial to the left and then to the right. Light the geyser and stand back." On a shelf beside the bath was a box of long matches.

Josie returned to her room and changed into her dressing gown, found a pound coin, and went back to the bathroom. She put the coin in the metre and twisted the dial, then turned on the water. There was a hiss of gas. She fumbled anxiously with the box of matches, lit one, and poked it into the metre. There was a terrifying bang as the gas lit but the stream of water became hot.

The bath was old and deep and took about half an hour to fill. At last, she sank into it and wondered what she was going to do about Hamish Macbeth. Perhaps the village women at the church hall could fill her in with some details.

*   *   *

Hamish Macbeth crowed over the phone to Jimmy Anderson. "I'm telling you, I give that lassie two days at the most. By the time Mrs. Wellington's finished with her, she'll be crying for a transfer back to Strathbane."

Josie decided that evening to dress in her uniform to give herself a bit of gravitas. She still felt hungry. She was used to dinner in the evening, not the high tea served in homes in Lochdubh. She had eaten a small piece of fish with a portion of canned peas and one boiled potato followed by two very hard tea cakes.

To her relief, there were cakes, sandwiches, and tea on offer at the village hall. Mrs. Wellington introduced her all round. Josie wondered if she would ever remember all the names. One woman with a gentle face and wispy hair stood out—Angela Brodie, the doctor's wife—and two fussy old twins called Nessie and Jessie Currie.

Over the teacups, Nessie and Jessie warned her that Hamish Macbeth was a philanderer and to stick to her job, but Angela rescued her and said, mildly, that usually the trouble started because of women pursuing Hamish, not the other way around.

Josie tossed her newly washed hair. She had carried her cap under her arm so as not to spoil the hairstyle. She was angry with Hamish for billeting her at the manse and spoiling her dreams. "I can't see what anyone would see in the man," said Josie. "He's just a long drip with that funny-looking red hair."

"Hamish Macbeth is a friend of mine and, may I add, your boss," said Angela, and she walked away.

Josie bit her lip in vexation. This was no way to go about making friends. She hurried after Angela. "Look here, that was a stupid thing to say. The fact is I don't really want to stay at the manse. It's a bit like being in boarding school. I'm angry with Hamish for not finding me somewhere a bit more congenial."

"Oh, you'll get used to it," said Angela. "Hamish covers a huge beat. You'll be out all day."

The next morning, Hamish presented Josie with ordnance survey maps and a long list of names and addresses. "These are elderly people who live alone in the remoter areas," he said. "It's part of our duties to periodically check up on them. You won't be able to do it all in one day or maybe two. We only have the one vehicle so you'll need to use your own. Give me any petrol receipts and I'll get the money back for you."

Josie longed to ask him what he was going to do, but had decided her best plan was to be quiet and willing until he cracked. And she was sure he would crack and realise what wife potential he had under his highland nose.

She gave him her mobile phone number and set out, deciding to try some of the faraway addresses first. Josie drove along, up and down the one-track roads of Sutherland, lost in a happy dream.

The hard fact was that she should never have joined the police force. But a television drama, *The Bill*, had fired her imagination. By fantasising herself into the character of a strong and competent policewoman, she had passed through her training fairly easily. Her sunny nature made her popular. She had not been in Strathbane long enough for any really nasty cases to wake her up to the realities of her job. She baked cakes for the other constables, asked about their wives and families, and generally made herself well liked. She was given easy assignments.

Then one day after she had been in Strathbane only a few weeks, Hamish Macbeth strolled into police headquarters. Josie took one look at his tall figure, flaming red hair, and hazel eyes and decided she was in love. And since she was already in love with some sort of Brigadoon idea of the Highlands, she felt that Hamish Macbeth was a romantic figure.

Hamish Macbeth began to receive telephone calls from people in the outlying crofts praising Josie McSween. She was described as "a ray of sunshine," "a ministering angel," and "a fine wee lassie."

As there was no crime on his beat and Josie was covering what would normally be his duties, Hamish found himself at liberty to mooch around the village and go fishing.

During the late afternoon, with his dog and cat at his heels, he strolled around to see his friend Angela Brodie, the doctor's wife. Angela was a writer, always in the throes of trying to produce another book. She typed on her laptop at the kitchen table where the cats prowled amongst the lunch debris which Angela had forgotten to clear away.

"You'll need to lock your beasts in the living room," said Angela. "Sonsie frightens my cats."

"I'll let them run outside," said Hamish, shooing his pets out the door. "They'll be fine. How's it going?"

"Not very well. I had a visit from a French writer. One of my books has been translated into French. She spoke excellent

English, which is just as well because I have only school French. I think I upset her."

"How?"

"Pour yourself some coffee. It's like this. She talked about the glories of being a writer. She said it was a spiritual experience. She said this must be a marvellous place for inspiration. Well, you know, writers who wait for inspiration get mental block. One just slogs on. I said so. She got very high and mighty and said I could not be a real writer. She said, 'Pouf!'"

"Meaning?"

"It's that sort of sound that escapes the French mouth when they make a moue of contempt."

"I haven't seen a tourist here in ages," said Hamish, sitting down opposite her. "The Americans can't afford to come this far and the French are tied up in the credit crunch."

"By the way she was dressed, she had private means. I bet she published her books herself," said Angela. "How's your new copper?"

"Rapidly on her way to becoming the saint o' Sutherland. I sent her off to check on the isolated folks and they've been phoning me up to say how marvellous she is. Every time I go back to the police station, there's another one ringing in wi' an accolade."

Angela leaned back in her chair. "What's she after?"

"What do you mean?"

"A pretty little girl like that doesn't want to be buried up here in the wilds unless she has some sort of agenda."

"I don't think she has. I think she was simply told to go.

Jimmy said she had volunteered but I find that hard to believe."

"Had she met you before?"

"No. First I saw of her was when she landed on my doorstep." Hamish had not even noticed Josie that time when she had first seen him at police headquarters. "Anyway, as long as she keeps out o' ma hair, we'll get along just fine."

By the time the days dragged on until the end of June, Josie was bored. There was no way of getting to him. She could not tempt him with beautiful meals because Mrs. Wellington had decided not to let her use the kitchen, saying if she wanted an evening meal she would cook it and bill headquarters for the extra expense, and when, one evening, Josie plucked up courage and suggested to Hamish that she would cook a meal for them both, he had said, "Don't worry, McSween. I'm going out."

It wasn't that Hamish did not like his constable, it was simply that he valued his privacy and thought that letting any woman work in his kitchen was a bad idea. Look what had happened when he had been briefly engaged to Priscilla Halburton-Smythe. Without consulting him, she'd had his beloved stove removed and a nasty electric cooker put in instead. No, you just couldn't let a woman in the kitchen.

Josie had three weeks' holiday owing. She decided to spend it with her mother in Perth. Her mother always knew what to do.

Josie was an only child, and Mrs. Flora McSween had brought her daughter up on a diet of romantic fiction. Just before she arrived, Flora had been absorbed in the latest issue of *The People's Friend*. *The People's Friend* magazine had grown and prospered by sticking to the same formula of publishing romantic stories. While other women's magazines had stopped publishing fiction and preferred hard-hitting articles such as "I Had My Father's Baby" and other exposés, *People's Friend* went its own sweet way, adding more and more stories as its circulation rose. It also contained articles on Scotland, recipes, poetry, knitting patterns, notes from a minister, and advice from an agony aunt.

The arrival of her copy was the highlight of Flora's week. When her daughter burst in the door, saying, "It's no good, Ma. He's barely aware of my existence," Flora knew exactly who she was talking about, her daughter having shared her romantic dreams about Hamish over the phone.

"Now, pet," said Flora, "sit down and take your coat off and I'll make us a nice cup of tea. Faint heart never won a gentleman. Maybe you've been trying too hard."

"He calls me McSween, he send me off hundreds of miles to check on boring old people and make sure they're all right. I'm so tired of smiling and drinking tea and eating scones, I could scream."

"You know what would bring you together? A nice juicy crime."

"So what if there isn't one in that backwater? What do I do? Murder someone?"

Chapter Two

☠

The woman is so hard
Upon the woman.

—Alfred, Lord Tennyson

Hamish barely thought about Josie. He was cynically sure that she would not last very long.

Now that she was away on holiday, he could put her right out of his mind. He was not very surprised, however, that on the day Josie was supposed to be back at work, her mother phoned to say her daughter had come down with a severe summer cold. She said a doctor's certificate had been sent to Strathbane.

Hamish said that Josie was to take as long as she liked and sent his regards.

"What exactly did he say?" demanded Josie when her mother put down the phone.

"He sent you his very warmest wishes," said Flora, exaggerating wildly.

Josie glowed. "I told you, Ma, absence does make the heart grow fonder."

One of the real reasons Josie was delaying her return by claiming to have a cold was that, although she would not admit it to herself, she preferred dreams to reality. Just so long as she was away from Hamish, she could dream about him gathering her in his arms and whispering sweet nothings. He said all the things she wanted him to say.

But that message about "warmest wishes" buoyed her up so much that she decided to return in two days' time. "You don't think Strathbane will phone the doctor to check up?" she asked anxiously. Flora had stolen one of the certificates from the doctor's pad when he was not looking.

"Och, no. You'll be just fine."

So Josie eventually set out with a head full of dreams— dreams which crashed down to her feet when Hamish opened the kitchen door and said, "Hullo, McSween. Are you fit for work?"

Work turned out to be a case of shoplifting over in Cnothan. Rain was drumming down and the midges, those Scottish mosquitoes, were out in clouds, undeterred by the downpour.

The job was very easy. The shopkeeper had a video security camera and had identified the thief. "I'll go right now and arrest him," said Josie eagerly.

"Now, I wouldn't be doing that, lassie," said the shopkeeper. "It's just some poor auld drunk who took a bottle o' cider. I won't be pressing charges."

"So why did you drag the police all the way here?" demanded Josie angrily.

"I didnae know it was him until I looked at the video fillum."

The rain had stopped when Josie left the shop. She pulled out her phone to call Hamish and then decided against it. If she called at the police station to deliver her report, surely he would have to ask her in.

Sure enough, Hamish did invite her into the kitchen, but there was a woman there, sitting at the kitchen table. She was a cool blonde in expensive clothes. Hamish introduced her as Priscilla Halburton-Smythe. Josie knew from headquarters gossip that this was the woman Hamish had once been engaged to.

She delivered her report, saying angrily that she should have been allowed to make an arrest.

"Oh, we don't arrest anyone up here if we can possibly avoid it," said Hamish. "Take the rest of the day off."

Josie stood there, hopefully. There was a pot of tea on the table and cakes.

"Run along," said Hamish.

"You could have given her some tea," said Priscilla.

"I'm keeping her right out," said Hamish. "If she gets a foot in the door, before you know it she'll be rearranging the furniture."

"Where's she staying?"

"Up at the manse."

"How gloomy! She must be feeling very lonely."

"Priscilla, she's a grown-up policewoman! She'll need to

make friends here just like anyone else. How long are you staying?"

"Just a couple more days."

"Dinner tonight?"

"All right. The Italian's?"

"Yes, I'll meet you there at eight."

Unfortunately for Hamish, Josie decided to have dinner out that night. She stood hesitating in the door of the restaurant. To Hamish's annoyance, Priscilla called her over and said, "Do join us."

Hamish behaved badly during the meal, sitting in scowling silence as Priscilla politely asked Josie about her work and her home in Perth. She seemed completely unaware of Hamish's bad mood. Josie translated Hamish's discourtesy into a sort of Heathcliff brooding silence. Such were her fantasies about him that at one point, Josie thought perhaps he wanted to be alone with her and wished Priscilla would leave.

The awkward meal finally finished. Priscilla insisted on paying. Hamish thanked her curtly outside the restaurant and then strode off in the direction of the police station without a backward look.

Back in her room at the manse, common sense finally entered Josie's brain and she had reluctantly to admit to herself that it was not Priscilla that Hamish had wanted to leave but herself. She dismally remembered Priscilla's glowing beauty.

She decided to give the job just two more months and then request a transfer back to Strathbane.

*   *   *

The third of the Scottish Quarter Days, Lammas, the first
of August, marks the start of autumn and the harvest season.
Lammas perhaps had begun as a celebration of the Celtic god-
dess Lugh, and was absorbed into the church calendar as Loaf
Mass Day. Lammas takes its name from the Old English *half*,
meaning "loaf." The first cut of the harvest was made on Lammas Day in the south, but in Braikie in Sutherland—a county
hardly famous for its corn—it was an annual fair day to celebrate the third quarter.

For the first time, Josie was to work with Hamish, policing the fair. "There's never any trouble," he said as he drove
Josie there in the police Land Rover. "The Gypsies have to be
watched. Make sure the coconuts are not glued down and that
the rifle sights at the shooting range aren't bent. It's a grand day
for it."

There was not a cloud in the sky. It was Josie's first visit to
Braikie, her other trips having, apart from Cnothan, only been
to the remote areas. The town was gaily decorated with flags.

A peculiar sight met Josie's eyes as they cruised along the
main street. A man covered in flannel and stuck all over with
a thick matting of spiky burrs was making his way along the
street.

"That's the Burryman," said Hamish.

"What on earth is a Burryman?" asked Josie.

"Some folks say he is carrying off all the town's shame and
guilt, and others say it's good luck for the fishermen, because all
the burrs are supposed to represent fish caught in their nets."

He drove to a field north of the town where the fair was
being held. Hamish strolled around the various booths with

Josie, stopping here and there to introduce her to towns-people.

There was all the fun of the fair, from a Ferris wheel and roundabouts to candy floss, hot dogs, and venison burgers.

The Gypsies, having spotted the arrival of Hamish, made sure he had nothing to complain about.

Josie walked along with Hamish in a happy dream as the sun shone down and the air was full of jaunty raucous music and the smells of frying food and sugary candy floss.

"We're walking along here like an old married couple," said Josie.

Hamish stopped abruptly. "You're quite right," he said. "It's a waste of manpower. You patrol the left and I'll patrol the right," and with that he walked off.

Josie sadly watched him go. Then she saw a fortune-teller's caravan. She shrugged. May as well get her fortune told.

She entered the caravan. There was a disappointingly ordinary-looking middle-aged woman sitting on a sofa. She had grey permed hair and was wearing a blouse and tweed skirt and sensible brogues.

"Sit down," she said. "Five pounds, please."

Feeling very let down, Josie handed over five pounds. Where were the tarot cards, the crystal ball, and the kabbalistic signs?

"Let me see your hands."

Josie held out her small, plump hands.

"You'll live long," said the fortune-teller, "and have two chil-dren."

"My husband? Who's my husband?" asked Josie eagerly.

"I cannae see one. There's darkness and danger up ahead. Let go of your dreams and you'll be fine."

"Anything else?"

"Isn't that enough?"

"You're a fraud," said Josie angrily.

The Gypsy's light grey eyes flashed with dislike and then suddenly seemed to look through her. "Bang and flames," she said.

"What?"

"There's danger up ahead. Look out for bombs."

"Glad to know the Taliban are going to pay a visit to this dead-alive dump, this arsehole of the British Isles. It might liven things up," said Josie furiously. She walked down the steps of the caravan and stood blinking in the sunlight.

What a waste of five pounds, thought Josie crossly. Then she saw that the crowds were beginning to move towards the far side of the field, where a decorated platform had been erected. "What's going on?" she asked a woman.

"It's the crowning o' the Lammas queen."

Josie followed the crowd. It was very hot. She could feel the sun burning down right through her cap. This far north, she thought, there was no pollution to block any of the sun's rays.

In the distance she could hear the skirl of the pipes. Using her authority, Josie pushed her way to the front. The provost, the Scottish equivalent of the English mayor with his gold chain, was already on the platform surrounded by various town worthies. Hamish was there as well, standing to one side of the platform. She went to join him. A wide gate at the side of the field was being held open.

First came the pipe band, playing "Scotland the Brave." Behind came a decorated float with the queen seated on a throne with two handmaidens. The Lammas queen was a true highland beauty with black glossy hair and wide blue eyes fringed with heavy lashes.

The float was decorated with sheaves of corn. "Where did they get the corn?" asked Josie.

"Plastic," said Hamish.

The queen was helped down from the float, and two men in kilts carried her throne up onto the platform. The pipes fell silent. "What's her name?" asked Josie.

"That's Annie Fleming," said Hamish. "She works as a secretary ower in Strathbane. Her parents are right strict. I'm surprised they let her be queen."

Annie was wearing a white gown covered with a red robe trimmed in rabbit fur.

She sat down on the throne. To Josie's surprise, the crown, which was carried to the platform by a nervous little girl bearing it on a red cushion, looked like a real diamond tiara. The gems blazed in the sunlight, sending out prisms of colour.

"Is that real?" Josie asked.

"Aye," said Hamish. "It once belonged to a Lady Etherington, English she was, and right fond of the Highlands. She lent it out once and her family have got it out o' the bank every Lammas Day since then."

"Do the family live in Braikie?"

"No. Lady Etherington's grandson who owns the tiara lives in London but he's got a shooting box up outside Crask and he aye comes up for the grouse shooting."

Gareth Tarry, the provost, made a long boring speech. It was mostly about defending the council's decision to stop building the seawall on the road to Braikie where, in previous years, the houses had been flooded at high tide.

It was only when an infuriated man from the audience shouted out, "You wouldnae be broke, ye numptie, if ye hadnae pit all your money in an Iceland bank."

Anyone who had invested their savings in Iceland banks during the credit crunch was currently left in doubt as to whether they would get their money back.

The provost pretended not to hear but decided to get on with the crowning. He raised the glittering tiara and announced solemnly, "I now crown Miss Annie Fleming the Lammas queen."

Everyone cheered. Annie graciously waved a white-gloved hand. She was helped down from the platform and back onto the float. Her throne was carried up onto it. The pipe band struck up again and the float, pulled by a tractor, moved off.

"She's off round the town," said Hamish. "You stay here and I'll follow and keep my eye on that tiara."

Hamish loped off. Josie miserably watched him go. She had looked forward so much to spending the day with him. But she suddenly had work to do.

People who owned houses along the shore road leading into Braikie, and who had been unable to sell their properties because of the frequent flooding from the rising sea, were gathering in front of the platform, heckling Mr. Tarry. He was a plump, self-satisfied-looking banker.

The provost saw the arrival of his official Daimler on the

road outside the field and, climbing down from the platform, he tried to ignore the crowd and make his way to it. "You listen tae me," shouted one man, and, trying to stop him, grabbed him by the gold chain.

Josie sprang into action. She twisted the man's arm up his back and dragged him to the side. "You are under arrest," she said, "for attempting to steal the provost's gold chain. Name?"

"Look, there's a mistake. I chust wanted to stop him and get him to answer my questions."

"Name?"

"Hugh Shaw."

Josie charged him and then proceeded to handcuff him. She heard cries of "Get Hamish," and "Whaur's Macbeth?"

Hamish came running back into the field. A boy had sprinted after him and called him back.

Josie said, "This man, Hugh Shaw, tried to steal the provost's gold chain."

Hamish looked down at her wearily. He knew Hugh owned a bungalow on the shore road. "Were you just trying to get his attention, Hugh?" he asked.

"Aye, that I was, Hamish. Thon fat cat has bankrupted the town, and until that wall is built there's no hope o' getting my place sold."

"Take the handcuffs off, McSween," said Hamish.

"But—"

"Just do it!"

Red in the face, Josie unlocked the handcuffs. Hamish raised his voice. "Now listen here, all of you. The only way you're going to get that wall built is to do something about it yourselves. There are out-o'-work bricklayers and dry-stone wallers amongst ye. We'll work out some fund-raising scheme and build the damn thing ourselves."

There was an excited murmur as the news spread back through the crowd. The local minister, Mr. Cluskie, mounted the platform and went to the microphone. He announced that Hamish Macbeth had come up with a very good idea to save the seawall. He said a meeting would be held in the church hall on the following evening to discuss ideas for the fund-raising. This was greeted with loud cheers. Then Hugh called for three cheers for Hamish Macbeth.

Josie stood off to the side. She was a small woman but she began to feel smaller and smaller, diminished, melting in the heat.

"The tiara!" exclaimed Hamish and set off at a run.

He knew that the tiara, when the procession reached the town hall, would be placed in a safe and replaced with a gold cardboard crown for the queen to wear for the rest of the day.

He jumped into the Land Rover and headed for the town hall in the centre. To his relief, Annie was being helped down from the float. The tiara was put back on the cushion, and Councillor Jamie Baxter took it off into the hall. Hamish followed.

"I just have to see it's in the safe all right," he said to Jamie's back.

"Och, man, each year you worry and each year it's fine. Sir Andrew Etherington'll be down on the morrow to collect it as usual."

Nonetheless, Hamish insisted on supervising the installation of the tiara in the town safe.

Then he returned to the fair and joined a miserable-looking Josie. After Hamish had run off, the crowd had shunned her as if she had the plague. "Let's go over to the refreshment tent," said Hamish. "We need to talk."

Josie trailed after him. "Sit down," ordered Hamish. "I'll get some tea."

He returned with a tray bearing a fat teapot, milk, sugar, mugs, and two sugar buns.

"Now," he said, "you have to use your wits. You have to understand the local people. Where those bungalows are on the shore road was once considered a posh bit o' the town. Then the sea rose and rose. They got flooded time after time. Times are hard and now the people who own these houses wonder if they'll ever see their money back. A good seawall would stop the flooding. The houses could be repaired and be sellable again. Tempers are running high. They feel the provost and councillors have bankrupted the town. It should have been obvious to you that Hugh was just trying to stop the provost."

"But he grabbed his chain! If that's not theft then at least it's assault."

"Look here, I go out of my way not to give normally respectable people a criminal record."

"What about targets?"

"I never bother about government targets. Do you want me to get like thae English—arresting wee kids for carrying water pistols and giving some child a criminal record for carrying a dangerous weapon, and all to meet targets?"

"But if you don't get enough targets, you don't get promotions!"

"I didn't even want *this* promotion. I want to be left alone. Now drink your tea, and if you are not happy with the situation get back to Strathbane."

One fat tear rolled down Josie's hot cheek, followed by another.

"Oh, dinnae greet," said Hamish, alarmed. "You'll need to toughen up if you want to keep on being a policewoman. It's not your fault. They'd love you in Strathbane for any arrest. Things are different up here." He handed her a soot-stained handkerchief which he had used that morning to lift the lid of the stove. He had to keep the stove burning if he wanted hot water from the back boiler. He had an immersion heater on the hot water tank but he found it cheaper to use peat in the stove because peat was free. He had a peat bank up at the general grazing area.

Josie sniffed and wiped her face with a clean part of the handkerchief.

"Drink your tea and we'll go out. Look as if you're enjoying the fun of the fair and folks will forget all about it. That Annie Fleming must be about the most beautiful girl in the Highlands."

"Oh, really?" said Josie. "Didn't look anything special to me."

Josie thought hopefully that by *enjoying the fun of the fair*, Hamish meant they should go on some of the rides together, but he ordered her to police the left-hand side of the fair while he took the right.

It was a long hot day. Josie had set her hair early in the morning but it was crushed under her hat, and trickles of sweat were running down her face. By evening, when Hamish briefly joined her, she asked plaintively when they could pack up.

"Not until the fair closes down," said Hamish. "There's sometimes a rough element in the evening." And he strolled off, leaving Josie glaring after him.

By the time the fair began to close down at eleven in the evening, Josie was tired and all her romantic ideas about Hamish Macbeth had been sweated out of her system. He was an inconsiderate bully. He would never amount to anything. He was weird in the way that he shied away from making arrests.

She sat beside him in mutinous silence on the road back to Lochdubh, planning a trip to Strathbane on the Monday morning, turning over in her mind the best way to get a transfer back again.

"You may as well take the day off tomorrow" were Hamish's last words that evening to her.

Hamish was outside the police station on the following Sunday morning, sawing wood, when he heard the shrill sound of the telephone ringing in the police office. He ran in and picked up the receiver. Jimmy Anderson was on the line. "You'd better get over to Braikie, Hamish. We'll join you as soon as we can."

"What's up?"

"Sir Andrew Etherington collected thon tiara from the town hall first thing this morning. He was on the way back to his home when there was a blast up ahead and a tree fell across the road. Four fellows he didn't know appeared and said they'd move the tree if he'd sit tight. Now Sir Andrew gets out of the car to go and help. He gets back in his car and waves goodbye to those helpful men. He's nearly at his home when he realises that the box wi' the tiara is no longer on the seat beside him."

Hamish scrambled into his uniform and then phoned Josie and said he'd be picking her up in a few moments. Josie complained that she was just out of the bath.

"Then take your car and follow me over," said Hamish. "The tiara's been stolen. Get on the road towards Crask. Take the north road out of Braikie and you'll see my Land Rover. Some men got a tree to fall over the road, blocking Sir Andrew's way, and when he got out to help them someone nicked the tiara."

Hamish was cursing as he took the Braikie Road. Every year the safety of that tiara was his responsibility.

As he drove through Braikie and out on the north road, he slowed down until he saw a rowan tree lying by the side of the road. He stopped and got out.

He remembered that tree, for trees were scarce in Sutherland apart from the forestry plantations, and such as survived were miserable stunted little things bent over by the Sutherland gales. The rowan tree, however, had been a sturdy old one sheltered from the winds in the lee of a hill that overshadowed the road. The bottom of the trunk had been shattered by a blast. He went across to where the tree had once grown and studied the blackened ground. He guessed a charge of dynamite had been put at the base of the tree.

He straightened up as Josie's car came speeding along the

road. He flagged her down and said, "You wait here for the forensic boys. I'll go on to the shooting box."

The shooting box was a handsome Georgian building, square-built with a double staircase leading up to the front door.

Hamish knew that the front door was never used so he went round to one at the side of the building and knocked. A grisled old man, Tom Calley, who worked as a butler during the shooting season, answered the door. "It's yourself, Hamish. A bad business."

"I'd like to speak to Sir Andrew."

"I'll take you to him."

"Has he got a shooting party here?"

"Not yet. The guests are due to arrive next week for the grouse. There's just Sir Andrew and his son, Harry."

"No other help but yourself?"

"A couple of lassies frae Braikie, Jeannie Macdonald and her sister Rosie."

Hamish followed him up stone stairs to a square hall, where the mournful heads of shot animals looked down at him with glassy eyes.

Tom led the way across the hall and threw open the door to a comfortable drawing room, full of shabby furniture and lined with books.

Sir Andrew put down the newspaper he had been reading. He was a tall, thin man in his late fifties with a proud nose, thin mouth, and sparse brown hair. His son, Harry, was slumped in a chair opposite his father. Harry, in contrast, was short and plump, owlish looking with thick glasses.

"This is infuriating," said Sir Andrew.

"Could you just describe to me exactly what happened?"

Sir Andrew went through his story again. When he had finished, Hamish said, "You don't have much of a description of the men."

"They were wearing those baseball caps with the peak like a duck's bill pulled down over their faces. They all wore sort of working clothes, grey shirts and jeans."

Hamish's eyebrows rose. "All wearing the same type of clothes?"

"Well, yes."

"What sort of accent?"

"Highland, I suppose, although one sounded a bit Irish."

"How Irish?"

"At one point he said, 'Faith and begorrah, 'tis a black thing to happen on a fine day.'"

"You're sure?"

"Would I make that up?"

Hamish glanced out of the corner of his eye at Harry. There was a certain rigid stillness about him.

"If you don't mind, sir," said Hamish, "I'd like to search the house."

"You need a search warrant!" shouted Harry.

"Go ahead," said Sir Andrew. "Pipe down, Harry."

Detective Chief Inspector Blair arrived followed by the scenes of crimes operatives. Then Jimmy Anderson along with a van full of police officers arrived at the bombed tree.

"Where's Macbeth?" demanded Blair.

"Gone to speak to Sir Andrew," said Josie.

"He should ha' waited for me."

"I've remembered something, sir. It's important."

"Spit it out!"

"I went to a fortune-teller at the fair yesterday . . ."

"God gie me patience."

"No, wait. She said something about a bang and flames."

"Oh, she did, did she? I might ha' known. Sodding Gypsies. I might ha' known they'd be behind this." Blair called everyone around him. "Get back to that fair. The caravans should still be there. Search every single one. Get it!"

Hamish met Tom in the hall. "Which is Harry's room?" he whispered.

"Follow me."

Up more old stone steps worn smooth with age. "This is it," said Tom, opening a door.

The room was dominated by an old four-poster bed. On either side of the bed were side tables covered in paperbacks. There was an enormous wardrobe. Hamish opened it. It was of the old kind with room for hats, drawers for ties and shirts on one side, and space for hanging clothes on the other.

"I'll leave you to it," said Tom.

"You'd better stay," said Hamish. "I might need you as a witness."

As he searched the wardrobe, he turned over in his mind what he'd heard about Harry. He had a reputation of being a bit of a wastrel. His mother was dead and Sir Andrew was rumoured to be strict, always finding some job or other for his son and raging when Harry usually only survived a few weeks in each.

The wardrobe yielded nothing sinister. He turned and surveyed the room.

Then he dragged a hard-backed chair over to the wardrobe and stood on top of it, his long fingers searching behind the wooden pediment on top of the wardrobe.

He slowly dragged forward a black leather box.

Chapter Three

☠

O Diamond! Diamond! Thou little knowest the mischief done!

—Sir Isaac Newton

Blair, originally from Glasgow, detested Gypsies even more than he detested highlanders. It was this, fuelled by his glee when Josie whispered to him that she wanted a transfer back to Strathbane and that Hamish Macbeth was useless, that caused him to make one of the biggest mistakes of his career.

He did not have search warrants but he ordered his men to search every caravan. The Gypsies howled their protests and then fell ominously silent. The reason for their silence was soon proved as no fewer than three lawyers, the sum total of the lawyers in Braikie, arrived, demanding to see the search warrants.

And as they were making their demands, Superintendent Daviot arrived on the scene.

Red-faced, Blair was just spluttering that it was a matter of urgency and that PC McSween had given them proof that the Gypsies were involved when Jimmy Anderson came hurrying up, clutching a mobile phone. "Hamish has just arrested Harry Etherington," he said. "He found the tiara hidden in Harry's room."

Daviot stared at Blair and then at Josie. "You, Detective Chief Inspector Blair, and you, Josie McSween, are suspended from duty pending enquiries. Where is Macbeth now, Anderson?"

"Taking Harry to Strathbane."

"I'll go there directly. Blair, make your best apologies and get your men to put everything back neat and tidy just the way they found it. Who is the head man here?"

"Me," said a small wrinkled man. "Tony McVey."

"Mr. McVey, you have our deepest apologies."

"Aye," said McVey. "And your damp apologies are not going to stop the lawsuit." He turned on his heel and walked away.

Harry Etherington had pleaded with his father not to press charges. He said it was all a bit of a joke and he'd got some friends up from London to help him. Sir Andrew simply looked at Hamish coldly and said, "Do your duty, Officer."

Hamish demanded the names and addresses of Harry's friends and learned they were staying at a hotel over in Dornoch. He phoned the Dornoch police and told them to bring the men in. Then he took Harry off to Strathbane.

He put Harry in a cell at police headquarters, went into the detectives' room, sat down at Jimmy's computer, and began to type out his report.

He was still typing when Jimmy arrived. "Where's His Nibs?" asked Jimmy.

"In the cells. Where were you?"

Jimmy explained what had happened and said that Blair and McSween had been suspended from duty pending a full investigation.

Blair marched past them into his office and slammed the door. Then Daviot appeared. "Come with me, Anderson," he ordered, "and we will interview Hetherington. First of all, Macbeth, what happened?"

Patiently, Hamish explained about having Sir Andrew's permission to search the house and how he had suspected Harry because of Harry's bad reputation and because he had been sure he was lying. Also, he said, Sir Andrew's description of the men—particularly the one with what had sounded a fake Irish accent—had alerted his suspicions. He said that the butler had been witness to him finding the tiara.

"Good work," said Daviot. "Do you want to sit in on the interview?"

"Och, no," said Hamish, not wanting to show any sign of ambition or desire to rise in the ranks. "I'll be off when I've finished this."

Daviot's temper was not helped because, before he could start the interview, Sir Andrew arrived and said he would not be pressing charges; he accepted that it had all been a joke. Harry's four friends were to be charged with possession of dynamite, malicious damage to a tree, and obstructing the road, thereby endangering drivers, and bound over to appear at the sheriff's court. Harry was charged not with the theft of the tiara but with conspiring to cause malicious damage and told he would be expected to appear in court as well.

Pondering the problem of Blair, Daviot wondered what to do. Blair was always attentive to him, and he was a Freemason and a member of the same lodge as Daviot. The detective always remembered Mrs. Daviot's birthday and sent generous Christmas presents as well. At last he decided it was Hamish's fault. Hamish should have phoned Blair immediately and voiced his suspicions of Harry before he had even begun the search.

Blair was lumbering out of headquarters when he saw Josie ahead of him, carrying a box of items she had cleared out of her desk along with a small potted plant. "Hey, you!" he roared. Josie turned round. Her face was streaked with tears.

"This is all your fault," said Blair, "and if you ever get your job back, you can rot up in Lochdubh until the end o' time."

Josie forced herself to speak calmly. "I told you what that Gypsy fortune-teller said, sir. I don't believe in the second sight. And where did Harry's friends get the dynamite from? One of the policemen told me some of the Gypsies had been working over at the quarry near Alness as few months ago."

Blair stared at her, his mind working furiously. Then he said grimly, "Get in the car wi' me, lassie. We're going to Alness."

When Blair discovered after two days of detective work that two of the Gypsies who had been working at the quarry had sold the dynamite to Harry's friends, Daviot breathed a sigh of relief. He would not need to get rid of Blair after all. Nonetheless, Blair had ordered an illegal search and the police enquiry dragged on for weeks. Josie was questioned and questioned until she felt she would scream.

When it was all over, and only a small amount of compensation had been paid to the Gypsies who'd had their caravans raided without a search warrant, she found that Blair had refused to give her any credit whatsoever. She was to be sent back to Lochdubh and consider herself lucky that she still had a job.

Had Blair been at all nice to her, had he given her any credit, had he asked for her to be returned to Strathbane, her old obsession with Hamish would have vanished like highland mist on a summer's day.

But all she could now think of was Hamish's brilliance in having found Harry Etherington out.

Hamish looked down at her with a flash of dismay in his hazel eyes. He wanted the village and his work back to himself. He told Josie to go back to checking on the outlying crofts and then got down to repairing loose slates on the police station roof. He expected a quiet winter and shrewdly guessed that Josie would soon grow bored with the long miles she had to put in, and ask for a transfer.

The winter arrived without much happening and Josie continued to doggedly perform all the dull tasks allotted to her. There seemed to be no chink in Hamish's armour. The Christmas holidays when she could go back to her mother in Perth came as a relief.

She poured out her woes to her mother who said comfortably, "There's bound to be a big case soon and then you'll be working together."

"Nothing ever happens up there," said Josie bitterly, "and nothing ever will. All Harry and his friends got was a slap on the wrist and community service. Those Gypsies got three months each. Harry and his friends had a top-flight lawyer."

Her mother put down the romance she had been reading. "There are aye a lot of blizzards up there in January with folks cut off. You'd be thrown together." Was that not what had happened to heroine Heather in the book she had been reading? And hadn't Heather ended up on a sheepskin rug in front of a log fire in the arms of the laird?

That was all Josie needed to fuel her imagination. When a really massive blizzard roared in, she would struggle along to the police station. They would be snowbound together, talking companionably by the stove. And then . . . and then . . .

But the winter proved to be unusually mild. Patel's, the local shop, began to show a display of Valentine cards towards the end of January. Josie longed to buy one, but was afraid Hamish would simply ask Patel who had sent it. Finally, she felt completely defeated. She would go to Strathbane and beg for a transfer, but after Valentine's Day. Maybe Hamish was cool to her because he was hiding a secret passion. Maybe a card would arrive for her.

Before going on her rounds on Valentine's Day, she hung around the manse until the post arrived. There was nothing for her. Determined now to get back to Strathbane, Josie bleakly set off on her rounds.

Annie Fleming, the Lammas beauty queen, did not go to work on Valentine's Day. She usually went to work as a secretary at a wildlife park outside Strathbane. She considered it a mangy park with only a few animals. It was the brainchild of an earnest English woman and her Scottish husband. It was the first job that had come her way and, as she was desperate to avoid working for her father who owned a bottle-producing factory, and to gain at least a little independence, she had taken it. On previous Valentine's Days, her father had insisted on examining her cards, demanding to know who had sent them. Annie had a pretty good idea who had mailed each card but, fortunately, the tradition of not signing cards was a blessing and so she had told her father she hadn't a clue.

But there was one she was longing for. A disco club in Strathbane had started lunchtime sessions. It was there that Annie had met Jake Cullen, he of the black leather outfit and supply of Ecstasy pills. In all her restricted life, she had never met someone more exciting. The drinks he plied her with and the drugs he gave her made her feel strong and confident.

She parked in a back lane in Braikie that afforded a view down to the main road. She waited until she saw her father with her mother in the passenger seat drive past and then drove home again and waited eagerly for the post. She knew her bosses were down in Edinburgh and that she was supposed to open up the wildlife park, but she persuaded herself that she would not be very late.

The doorbell rang. Annie swore under her breath. She had not wanted the postman to know she was at home. But there could be a really big valentine for her that could not fit into the letter box. She opened the door.

"Grand morning, Annie," said the postman, Bill Comrie. "Aren't you at work?"

"I think I'm coming down with something," said Annie.

"I've a rare bit o' post for you, and a package. You're popular wi' the fellows."

"Thanks." Annie snatched the post from him and shut the door firmly in his face.

The package was addressed to her. It looked exciting somehow. She decided to leave it until last. She had six valentines. Five were the usual soppy kind, but the sixth held a peculiar typewritten rhyme.

Roses are red, violets are blue
You'll get in the face,
Just what's coming to you.

Nutcase, thought Annie, putting it down with the others beside that mysterious package. Before she opened it, she went to the sideboard in the living room and took out a bottle of gin. She poured a stiff measure into a glass, carried the gin bottle into the kitchen, topped it up with water, and returned it to the sideboard. Back in the kitchen, she unpicked a little of the hem at the bottom of her jacket and picked out an Ecstasy pill. She swallowed the pill down with a gulp of gin.

Now for that parcel.

There was a tab at the side to rip to get the parcel open. She tore it across. A terrific explosion tore apart the kitchen. Ball bearings and nails, the latter viciously sharpened, tore into her face and body as flames engulfed her. Perhaps it was a mercy that one of the nails pierced her brain, killing her outright, before the flames really took hold.

Mrs. McGirty, an elderly lady who lived in the next cottage, heard the loud explosion just as she was about to enter her own home. She seized a fire extinguisher she kept in her car and ran to the Flemings' house and round to the back where she knew the kitchen was. She thought it was a gas explosion. The kitchen door was lying on its hinges. Screaming with fear, she plied the fire extinguisher over the horrible mess that had once been the beauty of the Highlands and over the flaming kitchen table. Then, white as paper, on shaking legs, she went to her own home and phoned Hamish Macbeth.

Hamish phoned Josie before setting out for Braikie. He did not expect her to arrive until later because she was supposed to be up in the northwest of the county. But Josie had become weary of home visits and so she had been parked quite near Lochdubh, up on a hilltop, reading a romance, when she received the call.

Hamish stood in the doorway of the kitchen and grimly surveyed the body. He heard a car driving outside and went out. Josie had arrived. "A murder!" she cried excitedly. "Where's the body?"

"In the kitchen."

"Can I have a look?"

"Go to the kitchen doorway but don't go in and don't touch anything. Suit up before you go in." Hamish was wearing blue plastic coveralls with blue plastic covering his boots.

Josie went back to her car and eagerly climbed into a similar outfit. Hamish stared after her, his eyes hard, as Josie went into the house. She was back out a minute later and vomited into a flower bed.

"Go and sit in your car," ordered Hamish, "and pull yourself together. I'm going to see Mrs. McGirty next door. It's thanks to her the place didn't burn down."

Mrs. McGirty answered the door. Her old eyes had the blind look of shock.

"I'll phone the doctor for you," said Hamish. "Go in and sit down and I'll make you a cup of tea."

He found his way to the kitchen, made a cup of milky tea with a lot of sugar, and took it to her. "Now you be drinking that," he said gently. "What's the name and number of your doctor?" When she told him, Hamish phoned her doctor and asked him to come along immediately. Then he said, "Tell me what happened."

In a quavering voice, Mrs. McGirty told how she had heard a bang and then seen smoke pouring out from next door. The kitchen was at the back of the house but the smoke was curling up over the roof. She had run in and plied the fire extinguisher.

"You are a verra brave woman," said Hamish. "If it hadn't been for you, possibly a lot of useful forensic evidence would have been lost."

There was a ring at the doorbell. Hamish answered it. He recognised another neighbour, Cora Baxter, wife of Councillor Jamie Baxter.

"Is she all right?" asked Cora. "Ruby? Mrs. McGirty?"

"She's in there. Could you sit with her until the doctor arrives?"

"I'll do that. Poor, poor Annie."

"How did you learn it was her?"

"Thon wee policewoman outside."

Josie should not be gossiping, thought Hamish.

When he went outside, the area had been cordoned off. The army bomb squad were just going into the house. The scenes of crimes operatives were suiting up. Jimmy Anderson approached Hamish. "They're saying it was Annie."

"From what was left o' the body, it looked like her," said Hamish.

"Who on earth could ha' done this?" said Jimmy. "I was talking to some folk at the edge of the crowd and by all accounts, they're a churchgoing, God-fearing family and Annie is prim and proper and a right innocent. And why wasn't she at work? The parents have been phoned. The mother works with the father. They said at first it couldn't be their daughter because she left this morning for work, but we got on to the postie on his mobile and he said he delivered the post to Annie. Said there were valentines and a package, all addressed to Annie."

"That's why she waited for the post," said Hamish. "She wanted to see her cards. Now, if she was that keen, there must have been a card she was really hoping for. Look, Jimmy, she worked over at that wildlife centre. I'll get over there and find out what I can. There's nothing I can do here until all the bomb and forensic evidence is collected. Where's Blair?"

"Got the flu. What about your sidekick?"

"I'd better take her with me."

        ✲   ✲   ✲

If Josie had been a friend, thought Hamish, he could have sent her back to the police station to look after his dog and cat. Angela had rebelled at taking care of them any more. Certainly there was a large cat flap in the kitchen door, large enough to allow both of them to come and go, but left to their own devises they were apt to go along to the kitchen door of the Italian restaurant and beg. Then they got fat and he had to put both on a diet and then they both sulked.

"Are you all right now?" he asked Josie as he drove her out onto the Strathbane Road in the police Land Rover. He had told her to leave her car behind.

"It was a horrible sight," said Josie with a shudder.

"What did you expect? She was blown to bits."

"I've never seen a dead body before," said Josie.

"You get used to it," said Hamish callously. "Once they're dead, it's just clay."

"What do you expect to find at this wildlife park?" asked Josie.

"I want to dig into the character of Annie Fleming. Her parents were very strict. Maybe she'd begun to rebel. Maybe she'd got into bad company."

Hamish turned up the muddy road leading to the park. A sign hung crookedly at the entrance. Hamish slowed to a stop and read the board. It said WILDLIFE PARK, PROPS, JOCASTA AND BILL FREEMONT.

They drove in past empty cages towards a hut with a sign saying OFFICE.

A woman came out to meet them. She was in her mid-thirties with two wings of fair hair hanging on either side of a thin face. She was wearing a shabby navy sweater over a grey shirt and jeans tucked into Wellington boots.

"Mrs. Freemont?" asked Hamish.

"I'll say one thing for you. You're quick," said Mrs. Jocasta Freemont. "I just phoned ten minutes ago." Her voice was upper-class.

Hamish turned and surveyed the cages. "Someone let them all out?"

"Exactly. Damn animal libbers."

"You say you've just discovered the vandalism," said Hamish. "Didn't you notice first thing this morning?"

"I've just got back from Edinburgh with Bill. That secretary of ours was supposed to open up."

"I'm afraid I didn't get your call," said Hamish. "Annie Fleming has been murdered."

"What! You'd better come into the office." She went ahead of them, shouting, "Bill! Something awful has happened."

A small man with a shock of grey hair was sitting at a desk. He rose when they all walked in. He was quite small in stature and wearing a grey flannel suit, silk shirt, and blue silk tie. Hamish wondered cynically whether the trip to Edinburgh had been to see some bank manager. He wondered why Jocasta was wearing working clothes.

"What's up?" he asked. "I mean, what's mair awful than some loons robbing us?"

"Annie's been murdered," said Jocasta.

"She can't be!" said Bill. "Who'd want to murder Annie? How did it happen?"

"A letter bomb," said Hamish. "I've a few questions to ask you but we'll concentrate on your missing beasts first. What did you have?"

"We hadn't much because we were really just starting up. Let me see, a pair of minks, a snowy owl, two parrots, a lion—"

"A lion!" exclaimed Hamish. "What on earth were you doing with a lion?"

"I got it from a circus. It was old. I think it'll come back round for food."

"What else?"

Bill gave a dismal little catalogue. Then he said, "I'm waiting for the SSPCA, and the zoo in Strathbane is sending some people up wi' tranquilliser guns."

"Look," said Hamish, "we'll need to put out a warning that a lion's on the loose."

He went outside and phoned Daviot. "I'll mobilise some men," said Daviot, "and tell the newspapers and television."

"Thank you, sir. I'd best get back to the Annie Fleming investigation."

Hamish hesitated before going back into the hut. It was an odd marriage, surely. Jocasta looked as if she came from a moneyed background whereas Bill was definitely lower down the scale and, from his accent, came from the south of Scotland. He wondered whether it was Jocasta's money that had set up this dismal excuse for a wildlife park. It was not on his beat—being covered by Strathbane—but despite the missing wildlife, he was sure the air of failure that hung over the place had been there from the start.

The sky above had turned a bleached white colour heralding rain to come.

There came a screech of tyres. First on the scene were officers from the Scottish Society for the Prevention of Cruelty to Animals. They'll never get their park back, thought Hamish. Even if all the beasts were found, those officers would take one look at the mangy cramped cages and shut the place down.

Then came Detective Sergeant Andy MacNab with two policemen. "I'll take over, Hamish," he said.

"I'd like to ask them about Annie Fleming."

"It'll need to wait, Hamish. Daviot's got his knickers in a twist about thon lion."

Hamish called Josie out of the office. "We can't do anything more here today. We'd best be getting back to Braikie."

He drove up the drive and turned off on the road leading back towards Braikie.

Josie felt hungry. "Could we stop somewhere for lunch?" she asked.

"We'll get something in Braikie. Heffens above!"

He screeched to a halt and Josie let out a scream of terror. A lion was standing in the middle of the road.

"I'll chust see if I can be talking to it," said Hamish.

"Are you mad!"

Hamish got out and went to the back of the Land Rover, where he had a haunch of venison given to him by a keeper the evening before. It was wrapped in sacking. He took it out and waved it at the lion. The great beast approached cautiously. Hamish tossed the haunch into the back of the Land Rover. The lion jumped in and Hamish slammed the back doors.

He climbed back in the front. "We'll chust be taking the lion to that zoo in Strathbane. I am not having the beastie returned to that dreadful park."

Josie wrenched open the passenger door and jumped out on the road. "It'll kill us."

"It's locked off in the back."

"I'm not getting in there."

"Suit yourself," said Hamish. He did a U-turn and sped off in the direction of Strathbane.

The zoo in Strathbane, he knew, was well run, unlike most of the rest of that dismal town. He wondered why he hadn't been met on the road, feeling sure that Josie would have phoned to say he had a dangerous animal in the back of the Land Rover. He did not know that Josie had found the batteries in her phone had died. He stopped briefly on the road to phone Daviot and say the lion had been caught.

At the zoo, the head keeper cautiously opened the rear doors of the Land Rover. The lion was asleep.

"I don't think the poor lion needs a tranquilliser gun," said Hamish. "I should guess it's awfy old. It came from some circus so it'll be used to folks."

Daviot had phoned the local papers, and several reporters and photographers were gathered.

"No flash pictures," ordered Hamish. "It's waking up. Let me see if I can get it out. Come on, boy. It's all right."

The lion blinked at him and slowly rose to its feet. The remains of the haunch of venison were lying beside it. "Now then," cooed Hamish. "That's the ticket. Slowly now. Just one wee jump. There we are."

The lion stood beside him. The keeper said, "Maybe if you follow me to the cage, it'll follow you."

"It had better be a good big cage," said Hamish.

"Och, it leads onto a bit of a field and a big auld tree," said the keeper.

Hamish followed him and the lion followed Hamish. Once at the cage, Hamish walked into it with the lion behind him. The keeper opened a sack he had been carrying and threw a lump of meat into the cage.

The lion fell on it and Hamish slowly exited the cage. "Turn those lights off," snarled Hamish at a television crew, "and give the lion a bit o' peace."

Hamish drove back to the wildlife park. The rain had begun to fall. Josie was standing outside the office, looking wet and miserable.

"They wouldn't let me in the office," complained Josie. "They said there wasn't room and I wasn't on the case."

"Get in," said Hamish. Josie meekly climbed in. "Now, what were you about, McSween," said Hamish. "Thon lion was secure in the back. It's where we put a prisoner, see? It couldnae have got at us."

"I was scared," mumbled Josie.

Hamish had been frightened as well but Josie did not know him well enough to understand that Hamish's accent became more highland and sibilant when he was afraid. But overcoming Hamish's fear was a desire to keep this noble old lion alive.

He was sure if Strathbane police had arrived on the scene, then they would have shot it.

"We'll say no more about it," said Hamish. "I'll switch on the heater. Do you want to go home and change?"

"I've only got the one uniform," said Josie. "I'll soon dry out. What are we going to do in Braikie?"

"I'm going to try to find out the names of some of Annie's friends. I want to know whether she had met anyone who might wish her harm. But maybe we'll begin at the post office and see if Georgie Braith, the new postmistress, can remember names of men or boys who bought valentines."

"Isn't it 'postperson'?" asked Josie.

"We aren't PC up here."

Hamish parked in front of the post office. "Could we have something to eat first?" pleaded Josie.

"Time's getting on. Stick it out for a bit." He looked down at Josie's dismal face. "Tell you what. You get something to eat. There's the fish-and-chip shop over there. I'll let you know if I find out anything. Meet me back at the Land Rover."

Why did Josie stay on? wondered Hamish. He suspected she had given up going on calls. Why didn't she just go back to Strathbane?

Georgie Braith was a tall, rangy woman with iron-grey hair and a beak of a nose. To Hamish's questions, she replied, "The parcel wasn't posted from here. I can tell you that. And how can I remember who bought valentines? It's age. I can remember twenty years ago but don't ask me about yesterday."

"Did you know Annie Fleming?"

"Of course. You know what it's like in Braikie. Everyone knows everyone else."

"What did you think of her?"

"A very bonnie lass."

"Do you happen to know who her friends were?"

"I remember now. She came in to look at valentines with Jessie Cormack."

"Where will I find Jessie Cormack?"

"She works as a secretary up at the town hall—the building department."

Hamish was just making his way out to the car when his attention was caught by a newspaper poster outside the newsagents. TV PRESENTER TO WED seemed to scream at him.

He went in to the newsagents and bought a copy of the *Daily Bugle*. He flipped open the pages and there it was: a photo of a smiling Elspeth Grant on the arm of a handsome man stared out at him. He read, "Our very own Elspeth Grant is to wed Paul Darby, heartthrob of the hospital soap *Doctors in Peril*." His eyes skittered over the black print. Paul Darby was English, and the couple had met when Elspeth was on holiday in the Maldives.

Hamish stood there, feeling forlorn. He remembered all the times he had been on the point of proposing to Elspeth but something had always seemed to get in the way. A voice in his head sneered, "If you had been that keen, you'd have proposed." But he felt depressed.

He put the newspaper in the rubbish bin outside and joined Josie in the Land Rover. "We're off to the town hall," said Hamish. "One of the secretaries there was a friend o' Annie."

"Anything the matter?" asked Josie, glancing sideways at his grim face.

"Nothing at all," snapped Hamish.

Jessie Cormack was a tall, thin girl with brown hair pulled back in a ponytail. Her eyes were light grey in a pale face. Her mouth, however, was wide and sensual although free of lipstick.

The town hall was one of those red sandstone mock castles so beloved by the Victorians. Jessie's little room was small and dark, separated from that of her boss by a plywood partition. It was very quiet. The thick walls blocked out all sounds from outside. The rain had turned to snow, and feathery flakes floated down outside the window.

"Do you know of anyone who might have wanted to wish Annie harm?" asked Hamish.

"No. Annie was popular with everyone."

Hamish was sitting opposite her desk. Josie had taken a chair against the wall next to a radiator. Hamish leaned back in his chair and said quietly, "The time for lying is past, Jessie."

Jessie studied her hands in her lap. Then she said, "Her parents will be mad."

"It doesn't matter what her parents think, and they can't get mad wi' a dead body," said Hamish brutally. "Out with it!"

"Well, it was like how she said the Freemonts who run the wildlife park didn't have a clue how to go on. She said they were losing money hand over fist. It was all Bill Freemont's fault. It was his dream and his wife's money. Anyway, they tried to get Annie to do some work round the cages, cleaning and that, but Annie said she was employed as a secretary and that was that.

"One day recently she heard Mrs. Freemont shouting that they didn't need a secretary because there wasn't enough work but Bill said they needed someone to answer the phones and take money from people when they weren't there.

"When they went off somewhere, Annie would lock up at lunchtime and go to that disco, Stardust, in Strathbane. They have a lunchtime session. She said she met a dreamboat there."

"Name?"

"Jake something or other. She was going to take me there one Saturday and introduce me."

"Anyone else?"

"She said Bill Freemont had come on to her but she threatened to tell his wife and he backed off. Och, it was her parents' fault. They were that strict. You know, church and Bible classes on the Sunday."

"Which church?"

"The Free Presbyterian Church in Braikie."

"So Annie liked to rebel?"

"She was a bit of a flirt."

"Oh, she was, was she?" said Hamish. "You seem to be taking her murder calmly."

"She was asking for it," said Jessie in a burst of sudden anger. "She flirted with my boyfriend and then laughed in his face when he tried to ask her out. He didn't have any time for me. He followed her around like a dog."

"Name?"

"Percy Stane."

"And where does he work?"

"Waste disposal. Across the hall."

"Right." Hamish got to his feet. "Did you get all that, McSween?"

Josie blushed. She had been daydreaming.

Hamish sighed and took out his notebook. "Right, Jessie, I'll need you to go over it again."

Percy Stane—what misguided parent called a child Percy these days? wondered Hamish—turned out to be a spotty youth of nineteen years. He had thick glasses through which pale blue eyes stared at them like a rabbit caught in the headlights.

"We just want to ask you a few questions about Annie Fleming," said Hamish. "Did you send her a valentine?"

Percy's eyes darted this way and that. "We have good forensic evidence," said Hamish severely, hoping Percy would think his card had been found.

"I-I d-did s-send one," he stammered.

"Now, that's all right," said Hamish soothingly. "You didn't send her a parcel?"

Hamish's mobile phone rang. "Excuse me," he said. He answered it. It was Jimmy. "Thought you'd like to hear the latest. At the autopsy, they found tablets of Ecstasy sewn into the hem of her jacket. It fortunately hadnae been burnt, thanks to that McGirty woman."

"I've just learned she had been frequenting a disco called Stardust in her lunch break," said Hamish.

"Good man. I've been dying for an excuse to raid that place for ages."

Jimmy rang off.

Hamish went and sat down facing Percy again. "Did you say anything in your valentine?"

Percy blushed deep red. "Do I have to tell you?"

"Yes."

"I didn't put a poem. I just wrote, 'Come back to me. Love, Percy.'"

"So she had been your date?"

"Not exactly." Percy wriggled in his hard chair. "Annie was always flirting and I thought she fancied me. I couldn't look at my girlfriend after Annie came on to me. I thought about her night and day."

"You mean Jessie Cormack?"

"Yes."

"Didn't it strike you as rather mean that Annie would flirt with you and then turn cold when she'd got you away from her friend?"

"I was . . . dazzled."

"Did you follow her?"

He hung his head.

"Come on, laddie. Out wi' it!"

"I called in sick one day and went to the wildlife park. As I approached, she was just driving off. I followed. She went to a disco. I followed her in. She was over at the bar with some low-life, laughing and drinking. I went up to her and she threw her head back and laughed. I said, 'What about a dance, Annie?' and her face went all hard and the fellow with her said, 'Bugger off or I'll glass your face.'"

"What did he look like?"

"Greasy hair, black eyes, leather jacket, tattoo of a snake on his wrist, and a bit older than her. He frightened me. I got out of there. I was determined to stay clear of her, but after a few days, I . . . I . . ."

"You followed her again?"

"I waited outside her house one morning to try to speak to her but she said if I didn't leave her alone, she would call the police. That frightened me. My valentine—well, it was one last desperate try."

"Did you see her with any other man, other than this fellow at the disco?"

He shook his head.

"Did you know she took drugs?"

Percy looked shocked. "She couldn't, she wouldn't . . ."

"She did," said Hamish flatly. "I'll be talking to you again."

Out in the hall again, Hamish said, "Back to Jessie."

"How did you know she took drugs?" asked Josie.

Hamish told her what Jimmy Anderson had said. He opened the door to Jessie's office. She was sitting at her computer typing busily.

"Stop for a minute," ordered Hamish. "Did you know that Annie took drugs?"

"No!"

"Never talked about it? Never hinted?"

"Not a word."

"I'll be back to see you. Here's my card. If you can think of anything, phone me up. There may be something you've forgotten."

*   *   *

Hamish dropped Josie off at her car. "I'm going back to Loch-dubh," he said. "You may as well get home and change. Take it easy. The snow's still light but it could get heavy any moment."

Josie drove off, peering through the windscreen as the hypnotic flakes swirled and danced in front of her. At the manse, she changed into civilian clothes and brushed down her uniform and then went down to the kitchen to borrow an iron and an ironing board from Mrs. Wellington.

"You've had an exciting day," said the minister's wife. "Hamish is quite the hero. I saw him on the television rescuing that lion. Were you frightened?"

"All in the day's work," said Josie.

Chapter Four

☠

I have spread my dreams under your feet;
Tread softly because you tread on my dreams.

—W. B. Yeats

Jimmy called at the police station that evening. "You'll never get back," said Hamish. "The snow's coming down thick and fast."

"You may as well put me up for the night," said Jimmy. "I've got to be in Braikie first thing in the morning. What a waste of time. We raided the disco. Clean as a whistle."

"I might go over there myself tomorrow for the lunchtime session," said Hamish. "I'm looking for someone called Jake."

"You've been on the telly. Everyone will recognise you."

"I'll go in disguise."

"You'll be poaching on Blair's territory."

"Then don't tell him."

"So what do you do if you find Jake?"

"Try to find out where he lives and give you the information. I might take McSween."

"How's that going, Hamish?"

"I don't know why that one ever wanted to be a policewoman. She hasn't a clue. Anyway, help yourself to a dram and I'll call her."

Josie had just finished speaking to her mother when her phone rang again. She listened to Hamish's suggestion that they go to the disco tomorrow if the snow allowed them to travel to Strathbane.

Her eyes were once more full of dreams as she rang off. Her mother had seen Hamish on television and was loud in her praise. Hamish began to appear a heroic figure in Josie's mind. He had said he would be in disguise but she needn't bother: just wear something suitable for a disco. They would dance, he would hold her in his arms, he would say . . .

"Are you finished with that iron?" said Mrs. Wellington, coming into the kitchen.

The countryside looked like an old-fashioned Christmas card when Hamish collected Josie the following day. Blair's desire to keep Hamish out of every investigation meant that he was not constantly being given orders or monitored.

Josie barely recognised Hamish. He had a false ginger beard and moustache and small John Lennon–type glasses. His flaming hair was hidden under a black wool cap.

She thought he looked awful.

*   *   *

The music blaring from the disco when they arrived was so loud that as they walked towards the club, Hamish was sure he could hear the beat reverberating through his shoes.

Inside the club, Josie took off her enveloping fun-fur coat to reveal that she was wearing a short red leather skirt, fishnet stockings, and a gauzy glittery blouse with a plunging neckline. She took off her boots and slipped on a pair of high-heeled red stilettos. Josie was also heavily made up.

They moved onto the dance floor. Josie was a good dancer but to her dismay, Hamish danced like a demented stork. A young man came up and began to dance with Josie, cutting Hamish out. Hamish gave her a quick nod to say it was all right and made his way to the bar. "I'm looking for Jake," he shouted to the barman.

"Ower there," the barman shouted back, pointing to a man in a black leather jacket at the end of the bar.

Hamish approached Jake. He tapped him on the shoulder and flashed a thick wad of what appeared to be fifty-pound notes. Actually it was one fifty-pound note wound round paper. "Come outside," he said. "I've a big deal for ye."

On the way out, he tried to signal to Josie. But Josie was lost in the music, her eyes closed, her hips swaying.

Outside, Hamish flashed his warrant card and said, "I would like you . . ."

But that was as far as he got. Jake took to his heels and ran but skidded in the snow and went down heavily. Hamish handcuffed him and hauled him to his feet. He realised if he phoned Jimmy, it would take Jimmy an hour to get from Braikie to Strathbane. He'd just need to take him to police headquarters.

Where the hell was Josie? He shrugged. He couldn't waste time going back for her, and Jake could have friends in the disco who might cause a fight.

Hamish had Jake searched at police headquarters and found he was carrying a good supply of Ecstasy and heroin. He had him put in a cell after being charged with possession. Then he phoned Jimmy.

Blair was sitting in his car, eating a mutton pie, when Jimmy told him the news. Blair let out a string of oaths, ending up by saying he would have Macbeth's guts for garters for poaching on Strathbane's beat.

"Maybe," said Jimmy. "But this Jake Cullen sounds like Annie's boyfriend, and she did have Ecstasy tablets on her when she was killed."

To Jimmy's surprise, Blair said, "I've got work to do. Get yourself ower there and keep in touch."

The owner of Stardust, Barry Fitzcameron, was a friend of Blair's. Barry also owned a couple of pubs where there were always free drinks for the detective inspector. Blair had tipped him off about the raid. When Jimmy had gone, he decided to find a public phone box and call Barry.

Hamish sat in on the questioning. To his surprise, Jake seemed quite cocky. He denied supplying Annie with drugs and denied having had any relationship with her whatsoever.

Hamish said, "We have witnesses who can testify that you were intimate with Annie Fleming and supplied her with drugs.

And don't tell me the quantity we found on you was for your own use."

"Look, I'm popular wi' the lassies," said Jake. "I may have given her a leg over. There are so many, I can't remember."

"Stop havering, laddie," shouted Jimmy. "Annie Fleming was the most beautiful girl in the Highlands. Nobody could forget her."

But Jake continued to stonewall until his lawyer was allowed in. He was told to appear in the sheriff's court in the morning. He was charged with having possession of and supplying drugs, and led away to the cells.

Blair got on the phone in a call box and phoned Barry Fitzcameron. "Thon numptie, Jake, has got himself arrested," he said.

"Has he now," said Barry. "Don't worry about him. I'll see to him."

"Where's your sidekick?" asked Jimmy as he walked Hamish to the door.

"I couldnae hang around waiting for her. Jimmy, do me a favour and get her transferred back."

"I'll see what I can do. Oh, there's the lassie, waiting for you."

Josie was slumped in a chair in the reception area. Hamish opened his mouth to blast her for having been so absorbed in dancing that she had forgotten her duties, but then decided wearily it was a waste of time.

"I'm sorry," babbled Josie. "I heard you arrested Jake. I looked round and you'd gone."

"I'll take you back, McSween," said Hamish wearily. "Chust don't say a word."

He dropped Josie off at the manse and told her to take the rest of the day off. Looking along the waterfront, he saw the press outside the police station. He guessed they wanted quotes about the lion. He did a U-turn and drove first to the Italian restaurant where he found his pets in the kitchen, collected them, and drove to the Tommel Castle Hotel.

Priscilla was crossing the reception area when he arrived. "Still here?" asked Hamish.

"Leaving tomorrow. I read in the papers about Elspeth getting engaged."

"Good luck to her," said Hamish with badly pretended indifference. "I've escaped up here to get away from the press. They probably want quotes about thon lion."

"I should think they're there to ask you about the murder. Blair killed the lion story. He's quoted on the radio and television saying the lion was very old, nearly dead, and a child could have rescued it."

"He doesn't know he's done me a favour," said Hamish. "Too much favourable publicity and Daviot'll have me off to Strathbane. I'd like to talk about it for a bit. My head's in a muddle."

"Mr. Johnson's away. Come in to the office and have some coffee. Yes, you can fetch the cat and dog in if you want."

Settled in the office with Sonsie and Lugs at his feet, Hamish told her all he knew about the case. He ended by saying, "I thought it would be easier. But it turns out that Annie was a bit of a goer, to put it politely, and God only knows how many men have got their knickers in a twist over her. I haven't talked to the parents. Maybe I'll try them when Blair has finished with them. The father's awfy strict. I 'member hearing that."

"You mean God might have told him to bump off his harlot of a daughter?"

"No. He wouldn't have sent something so elaborate as a letter bomb."

"Does it take a lot of skill to make a letter bomb?"

"The bomb's not hard. It's aluminium powder and iron, I think. But the skill comes in making the fuse and making it all so cleverly that it won't go off in the post sorting office."

"So you should be looking for someone with a terrorist background or someone with a good knowledge of chemistry? What about Harry Etherington? His friends knew how to detonate dynamite. Maybe one of them's got an iffy background. "

"Nothing showed up on the computer but a few drunk and disorderlies. Anyway, young Harry hadn't long arrived in the area. He didn't have the time to make Annie's acquaintance."

"What about the wildlife park? What's it like?"

"Hard to tell now that the animal libbers have let all the creatures out of the cages, but if the lion's anything to go by, I think the whole sorry place was a desert of mange and mud. Owners are Jocasta and Bill Freemont. Jocasta is posh and overworked. Bill is lower down the social scale."

"Bit of a rough?"

"Not that low down. A chancer and, I guess, a fantasist. I think he sold poor Jocasta some dream of the Highlands that only the lowland Scots on the tartan lunatic fringe know how to do."

Priscilla frowned. "Do you think this Bill . . . how old is he?"

"Older than her. Maybe getting on for fifty."

"I wonder if he or his father or anyone in his family were ever associated with the militant side of Scottish nationalism."

"There's a point. I think I'll pay them an evening visit." Hamish stood up and lingered by the office door. "I suppose I'd better say goodbye—again."

" 'Fraid so."

He moved a little forward as if to kiss her. Priscilla sat down abruptly behind the desk and began to shuffle papers. Hamish trailed out with his dog and his cat behind him.

He stopped on a rise on the road before the wildlife park and let the dog and cat out. He knew they liked playing in the snow and they needed to run off some of the fat they had gained by mooching in the kitchen of the Italian restaurant.

It was a bright moonlit frosty night. He smiled indulgently as Sonsie and Lugs tore through the snow.

It was on nights like this that Sutherland became a fairy county, all black and white, the silhouettes of the mountains rising up to a sky blazing with stars. He wished this murder could be quickly solved. Then he would concentrate on getting rid of Josie.

He called his pets, helped them into the back of the car, and drove to the park. He could see the lights were on in the office. Something made him switch off the engine and the headlights and cruise gently down the slope towards the office with the window open.

He slowly got down from the car and pressed his ear to the wall of the office. He heard Jocasta's voice. "I'm telling you. She said she saw you at Annie's house. It was one day a month ago when Annie said she was ill and you said you were going into Strathbane. She says you were in there for two hours!"

"If you're going to believe every malicious auld biddy in Braikie, you're dafter than I thought."

"Yes, daft enough to sink my money into this failure. I'm leaving you."

"Oh, come here, darlin'," wheedled Bill. "You know I'd be lost without you."

"But you went to her house!"

"I swear to God I never went near her."

Hamish thought he had heard enough. If one of the neighbours had seen Bill, why hadn't they told the police? Was it Mrs. McGirty? Or Cora Baxter?

He knocked loudly on the office door. Jocasta opened it. Her eyes were red with weeping.

"Have I come at a bad time?" asked Hamish.

"No, no, don't worry about me. I haven't been crying. Just some sort of allergy."

Hamish followed her into the office. There was a flash of fear in Bill's eyes, quickly masked.

"What kind of person was Annie Fleming?" asked Hamish.

"Ask Bill," said Jocasta. "I'm going up to the house. Good night."

Hamish waited until the door had closed behind her and then repeated his question.

"She was all right," said Bill.

"Did you have an affair with her?"

"What a question tae ask!" spluttered Bill. "And me a happily married man."

"Come off it. You were seen spending an afternoon at her house by the neighbours."

"I went to discuss the business wi' her. She's my secretary."

"Maybe you'll just be calling your wife to confirm that."

Bill crumpled. "Don't do that. Look, it wasnae me that seduced her. It was the other way around. I couldnae believe my luck, and that's a fact. It was just the one afternoon, that's all. Then she went on as if nothing had happened."

"When was this?"

"About a month ago. Please don't tell the wife."

"That I cannae promise. Do you have any training at all in chemistry?"

"Not a bit. Lousy at school all round."

"You'll need to stand by for more questioning. Don't go to bed."

Hamish went out to the Land Rover and called Jimmy. "What is it now?" groaned Jimmy.

"You'd best get out to the wildlife park and pull Bill Freemont in for questioning. He spent at least the one afternoon in bed wi' Annie Fleming."

"I'll get out there. What if he denies the whole thing?"

"I've got it on tape," said Hamish.

"Have you really? Or is that just one of your convenient lies?"

"No, I've got it all right. I'm off. I don't want to be caught poaching on Strathbane's territory. I'll wait for you at the top of the road."

Hamish waited patiently for what seemed like a long time before Jimmy turned up with Andy MacNab and two policemen following in another car.

"Right, Hamish, where's the tape?" said Jimmy. Hamish took a small, powerful tape recorder out of his pocket and handed it to Jimmy.

"Odd that," said Jimmy. "I never think of you as being high-tech. I wouldn't have been surprised if you'd written your notes up in the snow. Come on, lads. I'll keep you posted, Hamish."

The more she landed in disgrace with Hamish, the more Josie's obsession with him grew. As he was making his way back to Lochdubh, Josie sat in her room at the manse in front of the peat fire and dreamt of becoming his wife. In her mind, she remodelled the police station. There would need to be room for a nursery for the three children she planned to have.

It was only when she awoke in the morning with a hangover that she conjured up one sensible idea. If she worked hard investigating and maybe solved this case, Hamish would admire her. He would want her company instead of looking at her flat-eyed.

Hamish was relieved and surprised when Josie reported to the police station and suggested that she should do some investigative work in Braikie and go round the town and try to ferret out more of Annie's friends. Hamish filled her in with what he had found out about Bill Freemont.

Josie looked so neat and efficient in her newly sponged and pressed uniform that he offered her a coffee. Josie sat down happily at the kitchen table and looked around. It was a very small kitchen but could be extended. That old-fashioned stove would have to go. And the other thing that would have to go, she thought, eyeing the dog and cat who were slumbering together in front of the stove, was those wretched animals of his. She would get pregnant quickly and tell Hamish that his pets would cause allergies.

Hamish handed her a mug of coffee. "It's odd, isn't it?" he said in his lilting highland voice. "At first it seemed as if this murder was the work of some maniac. Now it turns out Annie was what Scotland Yard would call a murderee, someone who works people up so much that she's bound to get bumped off sooner or later."

"Or maybe it has something to do with drugs," said Josie. "I mean, Stardust, the disco owned by Barry Fitzcameron. He owns a couple of pubs as well. He plays the part of the good citizen, gives a lot to charity, that sort of thing. But when I was waiting for you at headquarters, I heard one of the policemen complaining about that raid on the disco. He said they couldn't even find an underaged drinker, let alone any drugs, and he thought Barry had been tipped off. Because one thing I did notice in that disco was that some of the drinkers were definitely underaged."

Hamish looked at her thoughtfully. He wondered why Blair

hadn't jumped at the idea of being there at the raid. "Which pubs does he own?" he asked.

"The Clarty Duck and The Stag."

"Interesting."

The phone in the office rang. "I wonder if I should answer that," said Hamish. "It's after nine and we should be at work. Better leave it." He cocked an ear as his answering machine picked up a message. "Hamish, this is Jimmy. Jake Cullen made bail. He was shot dead on the steps of the sheriff's court." Hamish rushed into the office and snatched up the phone. "You still there? It's me, Hamish."

"Did you get that?" asked Jimmy.

"Yes, any witnesses?"

"Only the one. Some poor auld granny has a flat opposite the court. A masked gunman came in the night before and told her to shut up or he'd kill her. He tied her to the bed. Then she said he just sat there, smoking and waiting. She thought he was going to kill her. Then she fell asleep. She said she was exhausted with fear. She awoke to the sound of the shot. Then he just ran out. It seems he set up at the window with a rifle—maybe a deer rifle—and shot Jake. It smells of a professional hit. And that screams at me that our oh-so-clean and worthy citizen Barry Fitzcameron might be behind it. We're going to be tied up here for a good bit. You and McSween get over to Braikie and see what you can dig up."

"On our way," said Hamish. He went back into the kitchen. Josie wasn't there. He walked into his living room. Josie wheeled around and blushed.

"If you want to examine my home again," said Hamish severely, "ask! Now let's get going. You find out what you can about her friends. Start off with the school. Maybe her messing about started there. I'll check back with the neighbours."

"I'm sorry," whispered Josie. "It's just I've never properly seen all round a highland police station before."

And never will again, thought Hamish. He ushered her out and then went out to his Land Rover followed by his dog and cat.

Josie drove miserably in the direction of Braikie. Before Hamish had caught her, she had opened the door of the spare room which led off the living room and had blinked in amazement at the amount of rusty junk. And he had just been beginning to thaw towards her. She was determined to work hard all day and not give up until she came up with just one clue.

Hamish followed her, his mind turning over thoughts about Blair. Then he mentally shrugged. It need not have been anyone as high up as Blair. It could have been anyone at police headquarters, down to the cleaners. If Josie was right, and there was underaged drinking usually at the disco, then it stood to reason that Barry had been tipped off.

The day was fine and cold. He slowed down on the shore road. Men were working on the seawall. The tide was out. They were working hard. He stopped and rolled down the window. "Got your funds?" he called to the foreman.

"Aye, but we can only work when the tide's out, otherwise we get battered wi' the waves."

Hamish drove on until he reached the quiet street where Annie had lived. He decided to call on Cora Baxter first. The councillor's wife answered the door. "Oh, it's you," she said. "Come in."

Hamish wondered at first if everything in the living room was new and decided he was looking at terrifying housekeeping. The sun shone through the glittering windows onto a glass coffee table where magazines were arranged in exact precision to line up with the edges of the table. The three-piece suite was in red leather, and the hair-cord brown fitted carpet was covered in hooked rugs. Hamish reflected she had probably made them herself. He had seen many like them at church sales. One bar was lit in an electric heater in front of the fireplace. The mantel was covered in little glass figures: he noticed a Bambi and a Snow White along with the Seven Dwarfs.

On a round table by the window was a cut-glass vase full of silk flowers. To one side of the fireplace was a large flat-screen television.

Hamish removed his cap and sat down on the sofa. The leather made an embarrassing fart noise. Cora stood in front of the fireplace. She was a stocky woman with bright blonde hair set in tight curls over a pugnacious face. She had small blue suspicious-looking eyes.

"Well, *Constable?*" she demanded.

Hamish repressed a sigh. From his experience councillors like Jamie Baxter, no matter how easy-going, often had wives who considered themselves a cut above the local community.

He stood up and approached her, looming over her. It had the desired effect.

"Oh, do sit down," said Cora. Hamish went back to the sofa, which welcomed his bottom with a loud raspberry. Cora sat in one of the leather armchairs, but the chair, no doubt knowing what was due to her dignity, did not make a sound.

Hamish opened his notebook. "I am making enquiries about Annie Fleming."

"Yes?"

"Did you phone Mrs. Freemont and tell her that her husband had been seen going into Annie Fleming's house to spend the afternoon with her? I must remind you that phone calls can be checked."

"Well, I felt it my duty," said Cora truculently.

"Do you know if this happened more than once?"

"I only saw him the one time."

"And when was this?"

"About a month ago."

"Any other men?"

"Just once. An unsavoury-looking character. He had gelled hair and one of those black leather jackets. I would say he was around thirty years old."

Jake, thought Hamish bitterly. That's a dead end in every sense.

"What did you think of Annie?" asked Hamish. "And did you tell any of this to her parents?"

"First, I did mention both visits to her parents. Her father was furious with me. He said his daughter was pure and I was a malicious woman who would burn in hellfire. Annie wouldn't burn anywhere, she was as cold as ice—butter wouldn't have melted in that girl's mouth. I saw them going off to the kirk a few Sundays before she died. Mr. and Mrs. Fleming put their noses in the air. But Annie turned round and gave me a nasty little smile before she walked on. I thought she was a devious tart."

"Why did'nt you tell the police any of this?" demanded Hamish. "You've been withholding vital evidence."

"I wasn't going to sully her memory until after the funeral."

"But you did just that by phoning Mrs. Freemont, and by trying to blacken the girl's name with her parents. Is there anything more?"

"No, but I don't like your attitude. Do remember my husband is a town councillor."

"Which means damn all in a murder investigation," said Hamish, and warned her he would be back to ask her more questions later.

Outside, he phoned Jimmy. "Any news about the murder?"

"Nothing. That old woman might have been left there till she died o' shock and starvation if we hadn't searched all the flats opposite and found her. She's in hospital for observation but she's a game auld bird and I think she'll survive the shock all right. He never took the balaclava off but she said he was pretty well built and wearing a black sweater and black trousers."

"Surely someone saw a man with a rifle running along the street?"

"From the initial SOCO report, he went down the stairs, out the back way, and over the wall. There's a lane that runs along the back. Neighbours heard a motorbike roaring off."

"If I were you I'd check out those two pubs of Barry's. See if Blair's been seen drinking in either of them. He likes his free booze."

"Aw, c'mon, Hamish. I don't like the pillock but this is going a bit too far. Don't worry. We're checking up on everything we know about Barry. Talk to you later."

Hamish wondered whether to interview the parents and then decided it was a bit early to subject them to more questioning. Blair would already have had a go at them.

He was about to get into the Land Rover when he heard someone calling, "Officer!"

He turned round. Mrs. McGirty was standing on her front door step waving to him. He went up to her. "Have they found out who did this terrible thing?" she asked.

"Not yet."

"You must find out. Annie was a saint and a good member o' the kirk."

"Maybe I'll be having a word with the minister."

Josie, meanwhile, was interviewing Annie's former head teacher, Miss Gallagher.

"Annie was a very bright pupil," said Mrs. Gallagher, a small, motherly-looking woman. "I thought she would be going on to university and interviewed her parents but they said that their daughter wanted to be at home and look after them."

"Were they ill in any way?" asked Josie.

"No, that's what was odd. They are both hale and hearty."

"Was Josie well liked at school?"

Mrs. Gallagher hesitated.

"I know you don't like to speak ill of the dead," said Josie, "but it is a murder enquiry and one of her boyfriends was shot dead this morning outside the sheriff's court."

"This is terrible. Just terrible," gasped Mrs. Gallagher. "To be honest, Josie did not have many friends amongst the girls. Looking the way she did, she was a great favourite with the boys but then even they began to shun her."

"Do you know why?"

"I'm afraid not. It's a terrible thing to say about the poor lass, but she almost seemed to enjoy her unpopularity, as if it gave her a certain power, as if she was looking down on all of them. I did send her to the school councillor."

"Why?"

"When a beautiful girl like Annie Fleming goes on the way she was doing, I begin to wonder if there might not be a certain trace of the psychopath there. If you go along the corridor, you'll find Miss Haggerty's name on the end door. I will phone her and tell her you are coming."

Miss Haggerty was a thin, frail woman with grey hair, spectacles, and a tired face. "Oh, Annie," she said in reply to Josie's questions about what she had thought of her. "I could not get anywhere with her. It was during her last year. She said she was looking forward to leaving the school because she found the other pupils too young for her. That was all she would say. She had good marks and seemed cheerful. Bright children often feel isolated, and Annie was very bright."

"Did you think she might be a bit of a psychopath?" asked Josie.

"Oh, no, simply highly intelligent."

"Manipulative?"

"I do not think she could manipulate me in any way."

Josie left the school feeling downcast. Her phone rang. It was Hamish. "I'm not getting anywhere," said Josie.

"I'm going to see the minister, Mr. Tallent. Like to come?"

"Where are you?"

"Outside her house."

"Be right with you."

Josie hummed a cheerful tune as she drove along. All was not lost. Hamish had obviously forgiven her for poking around his home.

Chapter Five

☠

Nobody who has not been in the interior of a family can say what the difficulties of any individual of that family may be.

—Jane Austen

"He may have been diddling her," said Josie as they both got out of the Land Rover at the minister's home.

"Who?" demanded Hamish.

"Her own father."

"For heffen's sakes, lassie, have you lost your wits? You've been watching *Law and Order Special Victims Unit*."

"It happens in these backwards places," said Josie defiantly. "Lots of incest."

"Look here, McSween, I don't want to pull rank on you, but I am going to. When we get in there, keep your mouth shut. In future, address me as 'sir.'"

Josie went bright red and hung her head, making Hamish feel like a pompous idiot. And yet it was time that Josie started behaving like a policewoman.

Hamish rang the bell of the manse cottage and waited. It was a two-storeyed Victorian sandstone building fronted by a garden full of laurels and rhododendrons on either side of a brick path. He pressed the bell and waited.

The door was opened by a squat man wearing black clericals and a dog collar. "I hope you are not here to bother the Flemings," he said.

"I didn't even know they were here," said Hamish. "It's you I want to be having a word with."

The minister led the way into a dark study, sat down behind a large desk, and indicated with a wave of his hand that they were to be seated in two chairs opposite. Hamish took off his cap and placed it on the desk.

"Get that thing off my desk!" snapped Mr. Tallent.

Hamish put his cap on the floor beside his chair. "I don't want any germs from your head on my desk," said the minister.

He had large angry grey eyes framed with thick spectacles. The skin of his face was thick, open-pored, and creased in folds rather than wrinkles. His grey lips were large and fleshy.

There was little of gentle Jesus meek and mild about the face opposite, thought Hamish cynically. This minister, he judged, probably preached a grand hellfire sermon on Sundays.

"As you know," began Hamish, "we are investigating the murder of Annie Fleming. Did you know her very well?"

"I am a great friend of the family. Annie was a beautiful God-fearing angel. Whoever did this will burn in hell for eternity."

"So Mr. and Mrs. Fleming are staying with you?"

"Yes, they could not possibly go back to that house until the police have finished with it and the kitchen is repaired."

"Was Annie particularly friendly with any member of your congregation?"

"I do not know."

"Did you know that Annie had been having a fling with her boss?"

"What do you mean? Speak plainly."

"She'd been having sex with him."

"Rubbish. Who is spreading this filth?"

"Her boss, Bill Freemont, admits to it. A neighbour saw him going in to spend the afternoon with her when she was supposed to be off sick. Annie also frequented a disco over her lunch break."

He thumped the desk. "I will not believe it. Annie Fleming was a saint." His eyes suddenly filled with tears. "Just get out," he said.

Hamish and Josie got to their feet and made their way out. They had almost reached the garden gate when a voice from behind a laurel bush whispered, "Psst!"

"Come out," ordered Hamish.

"Father will see me. Walk down the road a bit to the left and I'll catch up with you."

Hamish and Josie walked along to the end of the road. It ended at a scraggy field of gorse and tussocky grass, bordered by a dry-stone wall.

They were about to turn back again when Hamish saw a slight figure hurrying down the field, slipping and sliding on the frozen snow. A young woman came up to them, looking nervously to left and right. "I'm Martha Tallent." Martha had obviously come round some back way.

"The minister's daughter?"

"Aye."

She had a large nose which dominated her thin face. Her sandy hair was scraped back from her forehead. She was wearing a dark anorak over black corduroy trousers.

"So, Martha, what do you want to tell us?"

"I was listening at the door and I heard what Father said. It's not true. Annie was a right bitch. She hated the church. She told me. I thought we were friends. There's this boy who goes to our church and one day he asked me out. I was that excited. We were only going to have a drink in Braikie. I told Annie. She was the only one I told. She told my father and he came raging into that pub and dragged me out in front of everyone. We were only having soft drinks! That boy never turned up in church again. And someone told me he had been seen in a pub in Braikie with Annie. I'm sure she did it to spite me. But Father found out as well. I don't know who told him. In fact, Father blamed me and claimed I had been introducing his precious Annie to corrupting influences."

"What's his name?"

"Mark Lussie."

"And where does he live?"

"Down in the council estate. Culloden Way, number twelve."

"How old are you, Martha?"

"Nineteen. The same as Mark. Oh, if you see him, could you say how sorry I am?"

"Yes, I will. The Flemings are staying with you? What are they like?"

"They're grief-stricken. They and Mother and Father sit around of an evening talking about how good and beautiful Annie was. I've nearly finished my computer course at Braikie College and the minute I get my diploma, I'm going off to Glasgow to look for a job."

Hamish glanced along the road. He saw that a car had arrived; Jimmy Anderson was getting out of it, followed by a policewoman. Jimmy saw Hamish's Land Rover and looked down the road until he spotted him and began to walk towards him. Martha let out a squeak of alarm and scampered back off over the field.

"Who was that you were talking to?" asked Jimmy.

"The minister's daughter. But don't let on."

"Find out anything?"

"Nothing much except Mr. Tallent thinks Annie was a saint and furthermore, I think he had a crush on her. The daughter had a date in a pub and Annie told the minister and the minister descended on the pub like the wrath of God."

"We've now got at least a couple of witnesses to testify that Annie was a regular visitor to the disco," said Jimmy. "Mr. Tallent's just about to see his idol topple off her pedestal."

"What's happening about the shooting?"

"Blair's in charge of that."

"Jimmy, I think a leak came from headquarters somehow."

"We're checking. I'd best be off to see the minister. I've a feeling it's going to be nasty. You try your luck with that latest boyfriend."

*   *   *

Blair was sitting at a corner table in The Clarty Duck with Barry Fitzcameron.

"I swear I had nothing to do with the shooting o' Jake," said Barry. "I'm surprised an old friend like you could think such a thing."

"I phoned you and you said you'd take care o' it," said Blair. "I didnae mean kill him."

Barry raised his hands. "Would I do a thing like that? The silly fool was into drugs. Probably he didn't pay for the last lot."

Blair looked nervously around the bar and inched forward. "If it ever gets out that I tipped you off about the raid, I'm finished."

Barry looked the epitome of the successful businessman from his well-tailored suit to his barbered silver hair. "Nobody can find out. I didn't tell anyone, you didn't tell anyone, so what's your problem?"

"Let's jist say it's that lang dreep o' nothing, Hamish Macbeth."

"Oh, the lion tamer. What's he got to do with anything? Strathbane isn't his beat and you're in charge."

"He's sneaky. He poaches on ma territory."

"I'm telling you. Don't worry about it. Have another drink on me. Got to run."

Blair watched him go. Surely he had not arranged to have Jake killed. And yet he'd said he would fix it. What if he had Hamish Macbeth killed? A slow smile crossed Blair's fat features.

*   *   *

Hamish suggested they have something to eat. Josie's mind flew immediately to a corner table in a shaded restaurant. The balloon of her imagination was pricked when Hamish parked outside a fish-and-chip shop and asked her what she wanted. Josie stared moodily out of the Land Rover window at the large menu on a board: fish and chips, haggis and chips, deep-fried pizza slice and chips, deep-fried Mars bar and chips, chicken and chips, black pudding and chips, and sausage and chips.

"Fish and chips," said Josie.

Hamish returned with fish and chips for himself and Josie, fish for Sonsie, and sausage and chips for Lugs. He put the animals' food in their bowls at the back and then climbed in the front and gave a greasy package to Josie. He had also bought a bottle of Irn Bru, that famous Scottish fizzy drink which once had the slogan, "Made from Girders." It was an amazing success in Russia where it was advertised as a hangover cure. Hamish produced two paper cups and poured Josie a drink of it.

"I'll get spots . . . sir," said Josie gloomily.

"These are the best fish and chips for miles around," said Hamish. "Eat up and then we'll go and see this Mark Lussie."

When they had finished, Hamish collected up all the papers, put them in a bin outside the shop, and got into the Land Rover after wiping his greasy hands on his trousers. If only he'd let me cook for him, thought Josie. I'd show him what good food *really* tastes like.

Hamish whistled "The Road to the Isles" as he drove to the council estate. The day was clear and sparkling and for once, the dreaded gales of Sutherland had decided to leave the county alone.

A tired-looking woman with a squalling baby at her hip answered the door. She said she was Mark's mother and Mark was at work at the bakery. Hamish reassured her that Mark was not in trouble, then headed back into the centre of Braikie and parked at the bakery.

He asked for Mark at the counter. The baker looked alarmed. "I hope he hasnae been up to anything. He's a good worker."

"No, no. Just a few questions," said Hamish soothingly.

The baker went into the back shop. A few moments later, Mark emerged wearing white overalls and a white cap. He looked much younger than his nineteen years. He had a very white face and pale green eyes. He was small in stature, and his shoulders were stooped.

"Would you mind stepping outside?" asked Hamish. "Just a few questions."

"Is it about Annie?"

"Yes, I believe you were dating her."

Josie decided the time had come to show Hamish Macbeth that she was a real policewoman. "Did you kill her?" she demanded.

Before Mark could say anything, Hamish rounded on her. "Please go and sit in the Land Rover, McSween."

"But . . ."

"Just go!"

He waited until Josie had left and then said, "No one is accusing you of anything, Mark. McSween is new to the job. Let's begin again. I gather you were dating her."

"Aye. I couldnae believe ma luck. It was after Bible class one Sunday afternoon. She asked me if I'd like to meet her on the Monday evening for a drink. I said all right and she said she would meet me in the Red Lion. She started to drink vodka doubles wi' Red Bull. I'd never drunk alcohol before and what wi' her being such a beauty, I decided to start drinking vodka as well.

"I dinnae ken what idiot said that vodka didn't smell because my mother smelt it the minute I got home. But I didnae care because she had promised tae meet me the next night. We had just got sat down when her father burst into the pub and starts howling and cursing. Says I led his daughter astray. She didnae say one word to defend me. 'Forget it, Da,' says she. 'He's not worth bothering about. He's just some little fellow from the Bible class.' And that was that. I'm frightened to go back to the church in case the auld scunner accuses me of her murder."

Hamish left the bakery and got into the Land Rover. He looked wearily at Josie. "Policing in the Highlands," he said, "is not like a hard-cop American TV series. You deal gently wi' people and you'll get more out of them." He let in the clutch. "We're going back to the Flemings' house. Maybe something from the blast ended up in the garden and SOCO might have missed it."

Josie felt near to tears. It seemed she couldn't do anything right. She sat in brooding silence until they reached the Flemings' home.

It was still cordoned off with police tape. They both got out. "We'll go round the back," said Hamish. "As the blast was in the kitchen, there might be something blown outside."

The back garden consisted of a drying green with tattered washing still hanging on the line. There were a few bushes in the narrow flower beds that formed an edging around the green.

Hamish began to search carefully in the bushes by the kitchen door, and Josie began to look through the bushes on the left-hand side. As she worked her way round the garden, she grew cold and bored. The sun shone on the tattered washing. One of the items not too damaged was a serviceable pair of knickers. Josie suddenly noticed that there was something stuck inside the knickers. She went over to the washing line. The clothes were just beginning to thaw out. She unpegged the knickers. Hamish came over to her. "Found something?"

"Maybe nothing," said Josie. "But when the sun shone it looked as if there was a bit of paper stuck inside."

Hamish put on a pair of latex gloves and told Josie to do the same. He opened up the knickers gently. Sure enough, there was a scrap of paper. "We'd best take this down to the forensic lab in Strathbane," he said. "We don't want to risk damaging it."

Hamish's heart sank when he saw forensic scientist Lesley Murray, formerly Lesley Seaton. She had pursued him at one time and was now married to her boss, Bruce Murray.

"You can leave it with me," she said.

"If you don't mind, we'll hang around and see if there's anything important," said Hamish.

Josie looked about in disappointment. It was hardly a scene out of *CSI Miami*. The room was dingy with frosted-glass windows. A faulty fluorescent light buzzed overhead like an angry wasp. There was a cup of coffee on Leslie's desk with a skin of milk on the top. She had imagined the underwear being subjected to forensic scrutiny under high-tech machines, but all Lesley did was snip open one side of the knickers and with tweezers carefully extract a piece of scorched cardboard.

"There's some writing on it. Typewritten," she said. "It looks like part of a valentine card."

Hamish leaned over her shoulder and read:

"Rose are re . . .

"Violets . . .

"You're going t . . .

"Just what's coming to you."

"I'll telephone Mr. Blair and tell him about this," said Lesley.

"You better telephone Jimmy," said Hamish. "He's in charge o' the case."

"Right. You can go," said Lesley. "I'll see if I can get anything more out of this."

"We'll wait," said Hamish.

"I have other things to do," said Lesley crossly. "And may I remind you, you are nothing more than a village bobby and not in charge of this case."

Josie opened her mouth to make an angry retort but received a quelling glare from Hamish.

Outside, she asked, "Is she always like that?"

"Pretty much. Nothing sinister about thon underwear because that piece o' cardboard was obviously blasted there, but the bit o' message is something."

I wonder if he jilted Lesley, thought Josie, her senses sharpened by jealousy. Lesley was pretty. Priscilla Halburton-Smythe looked like a model from *Vogue*. It was all very lowering.

In the very north of Scotland, night falls around three or four PM in winter. Hamish wanted rid of Josie. She had certainly found that important clue. But there was something about her, a sort of cloying neediness, that got on his nerves. He was bewildered by the growing list of suspects. There are so many, he thought gloomily, it's beginning to look like the local phone directory.

After he reached Lochdubh, he dropped Josie off at the manse and then drove to the police station. He helped the dog down as the cat sprang lightly onto the ground with her large paws.

"You haven't had much exercise," he told them. "We'll go for a wee dauner along the waterfront."

Halos of mist were encircling the lamps, leaving black areas of shadow in between. He had a sudden feeling of being watched. He whipped round but there was no one there. When he turned back, the Currie sisters, Nessie and Jessie, stood facing him as if they had just been conjured up out of the ground.

The twins were spinsters of the parish, still alike in their sixties, both having rigidly permed white hair and thick glasses.

"Awful, her turning out to be a tart," said Nessie.

"Tart," echoed her sister, who always repeated the end of what her twin had been saying.

"How did you hear?" asked Hamish.

"It was Mrs. Baxter, the councillor's wife," said Nessie. "Herself was down at Patel's this afternoon. He's got a special on tinned salmon. She bought ten cans! I said, 'That's not very fair. You should leave some for us locals,' but she paid me no heed at all. So then I says, poor Annie Fleming, and herself whips around and says, 'Annie Fleming was a whore.' Just like that!"

"Just like that," echoed Jessie.

"Mind you, I did always think she flaunted herself a bit. When are you getting married?"

"Getting married," put in the Greek chorus.

"I have no intention of getting married," said Hamish. He stalked off.

Mark Lussie was not a baker. He worked in the bakery as a sort of odd-job man, carrying out trays of cakes, bread, rolls, pies, and buns to the shop from the back. He cleaned the windows, swept the floors, and cleaned the baking trays and the ovens, and all the time he dreamed of greater things. He no longer went to church. He had prayed to be married to Annie and God had let him down so God didn't exist. He wanted to get out of Braikie and go to Glasgow or Edinburgh, or even London. He had very little in his bank as he had begun to find comfort in drink ever since Annie had introduced him to alcohol.

He turned over and over in his mind everything Annie had said to him. And then like a lightbulb going on over his head as it did over the heads of the characters in the comics he liked to read, he remembered all of a sudden that Annie had said someone had threatened her and he remembered exactly who that someone was.

At first, he saw himself standing up in court in his best suit, giving evidence and being photographed by the newspapers when he left the court.

Then it dawned on him that such knowledge was money and money meant escape.

When he finished work, he went out into the yard at the back of the bakery and lit a cigarette, a new vice. He took out his mobile phone and, looking around to make sure no one was about, dialled a number he had looked up in the phone book in the bakery.

When the phone was answered, he asked to be put through to the person he wanted to speak to. "I know you killed Annie. She said you threatened her. Pay me two thousand pounds or I'll go to the police. You know the war memorial on the hill above Braikie? Well, be there at midnight with the money or I'll go straight to the police."

The voice answered in the affirmative and rang off. Mark stood there, his heart beating hard. He would go to London! Maybe he would be in a bar and this film star would chat him up and take him back with her to Hollywood. He would get away from his home where the new baby cried all night. What was his mother thinking about to go and have another child? And who was the father? She wouldn't say. Mark's own father had left his mother shortly after he was born. The church had been a comfort for a while on the long Scottish Sabbath days, but it had let him down in the presence of Annie and her father.

He went back into the bakery and collected four mutton pies which had got a bit bashed and so he was allowed to take them home. There will be no mutton pies in London, he thought.

Mark felt very nervous but he did not drink that evening. He was frightened of falling asleep. Before midnight, he crept quietly out of the house and made his way through all the sleeping silent streets under the light of a cold, pockmarked moon. The streetlights were switched off to save energy. The great stars of Sutherland blazed overhead.

He walked through the town and up the grassy hillock where the war memorial stood, black against the starry sky. He glanced at the luminous dial of his watch. Five minutes to go. He looked up at the sky and saw that the northern lights had started to blaze in all their swirling glory. He had only seen them once before. What was it they called them in school? The aurora borealis, that was it. He felt the very heavens were celebrating the soon-to-happen escape of one Mark Lussie. Then he heard the town clock strike midnight and tore his gaze from the magnificence of the heavens and looked down the hill to watch for anyone approaching.

He never heard the step behind him. A knife was thrust savagely into the back of his neck. Rough hands searched his pockets after he had slumped to the ground and took his mobile phone. Then his assailant crept away.

Mark lay dying as the lifeblood pumped out from the wound in his neck. As the lights of the aurora borealis moved and swirled across the sky, Mark Lussie finally went on his last great journey.

Roger Burton, Barry Fitzcameron's hit man, crouched behind the sheep shed up on Hamish's croft. He had instructions to make it look like an accident. But he planned to wait until

Hamish Macbeth was asleep, get into the station, and simply shoot him. It would be easy to get into the police station. He had noticed one of the fishermen knocking at the door, carrying two fish. When he didn't get a reply, he had felt in the guttering above the kitchen door, taken down a key, and unlocked the door. Then he had come out a few moments later, relocked the door, and put the key back up in the gutter. Because Barry had thought Roger meant to stage an accident and because the person to be killed was a police sergeant, he had paid him generously up front. Roger meant to do the deed and clear off to Glasgow.

He waited until Hamish came back and then waited until finally the lights in the police station went off.

He was just about to make his move when the northern lights began to blaze across the sky. He suddenly felt he should leave it—just take Barry's money and run. But he was a professional and he had a reputation to keep. No one in the criminal fraternity of Glasgow would mind that he hadn't staged an accident.

He softly made his way towards the kitchen door.

Sonsie awoke and pricked up her tufted ears. Because of the odd telepathy between the two animals, Lugs awoke as well. Sonsie sprang down from the bed where she and the dog had been sleeping and went to the kitchen door. Her fur was raised. Hamish was to wonder afterwards why Lugs had not barked.

They heard the key in the door. Roger loomed up in front of them. When he saw the two animals he raised his gun but Sonsie, the wild cat, flew up at his face and tore her sharp claws down it while Lugs bit his leg. He howled and dropped the rifle.

Hamish came running in. He picked up the rifle and ordered, "Stay there or I'll shoot."

He scrabbled in the pocket of his coat hanging on the back of the door and produced a pair of handcuffs. "Over on your back," he shouted.

Roger rolled over, yelling, "I can't see."

"It's the blood," said Hamish, clipping on the handcuffs. He grabbed his mobile from the kitchen table and called for help.

It was to be a long night. The deep scratches on Roger's face were tended to by the medical officer before he was judged fit for questioning. But Roger remained silent apart from saying he was going to sue Hamish Macbeth for the damage to his face. He would not say that anyone had hired him to kill Hamish. Hamish waited in the detectives' room because Blair would not allow him to be part of the interview. He had asked them to find out Roger's address so that the place could be searched before anything was destroyed but Blair had snarled at him that he was not in charge of the case and to type up his report.

When Jimmy finally appeared, Hamish said desperately, "Have you an address? We've got to get round there. There may be something in his place that connects him to Barry Fitz-cameron."

Jimmy rubbed the bristles on his foxy face. "I'm tired. We've been up all night, Hamish."

"Let's just do it ourselves," pleaded Hamish.

"Oh, all right. It's a house in Boroughfield, that suburb at the edge o' the town."

*   *   *

But when they got there, it was to find the blackened shell of what had been Roger's home being checked by a fire inspector.

"I'm sorry, Hamish," said Jimmy wearily. "We should ha' listened to you. Go home."

Before he went to bed, Hamish locked the door. As he fell asleep, he was dimly aware of Josie shouting through the letter box.

Josie was alarmed when she did not get a reply. She phoned police headquarters and learned of the attempt on Hamish's life. Then she was told to hold on. Police Sergeant Mary Southern came on the line.

"Get over to Braikie right now and we'll join you. A body's been found at the war memorial."

Josie scribbled a note to Hamish and pushed it through the letter box before driving as fast as she could to Braikie. Trails of dark cloud were streaming in from the Atlantic, and the wind had begun to rise.

She stopped in the main street, asked for directions to the war memorial, and then set off again. As she climbed the hill to the memorial, she could see that a small crowd had gathered. She pulled a roll of police tape and some posts out of the car and set off up the hill, shouting, "Get back! It's a crime scene."

The little crowd backed away as she secured the site. Then she went forward and looked down at the body. Here was no horror such as she had seen when she had viewed Annie's body. Mark Lussie lay as if at peace, his sightless eyes staring up at the windy sky.

"Who found the body?" asked Josie, walking back to the crowd.

A tall man stepped forward. "That's me," he said.

"Name?"

"Alec Templar. I wass up the brae looking after my sheep and I saw what I thocht was clothes by the memorial and went for a look. Poor wee laddie."

Josie felt the experience of being in sole charge of a murder case was very exciting, but it was short-lived. Police, detectives, and SOCO headed by Superintendent Daviot came hurrying up the brae.

Daviot glared at Josie. "Why aren't you suited up?"

"I was rushing to secure the crime scene," said Josie.

"Don't ever make such a mistake again. Where's Macbeth?"

"There was an attempt on his life last night and—"

"I know that. So where is he?"

"I think he must be asleep."

"Then get over to Lochdubh and wake him up. I need him here."

"I know the deceased," said Josie tremulously. "We interviewed him yesterday."

"Name and address?"

Josie gave them to him. "Shall I go and tell the parents?"

"Just get Macbeth here!"

Josie drove miserably back to Lochdubh and hammered on the police station door. She jumped as a voice behind her said, "There's a spare key on a hook at the back of the henhouse. He used tae leave it in the gutter, but he changed it. He telt it tae me the ither day."

She swung round. A small man in a very tight suit stood looking at her. "I'm Archie Maclean," he said. "Friend o' Hamish's."

"I've got to wake him up," said Josie. "He's wanted over at Braikie."

"I'll leave you to it," said Archie. "I only came for a wee crack."

Josie found the key and let herself in. She decided that instead of shouting to wake him, she would go into the bedroom and gently shake him by the shoulder. It was an intimate scenario.

She went into the bedroom. The dog and cat were at the end of the bed. The large cat arched her back and hissed while her yellow eyes blazed. The dog barked.

"Hamish!" screamed Josie, darting out the door and slamming it behind her before the cat could spring.

The bedroom door opened and Hamish stood there wrapped in a shabby dressing gown. "What's up?" he demanded.

"There's been another murder, sir. Mark Lussie."

"Make coffee," ordered Hamish. "This all gets nastier and nastier."

Chapter Six

☠

O woman, perfect woman! What distraction
Was meant to mankind when thou wast made a devil!

—John Fletcher

Josie took one look at the cheap jar of instant coffee on Hamish's kitchen counter and ran to Patel's to buy a packet of real coffee. Returning to the police station, she made the coffee in a pewter jug by pouring boiling water over the grounds, sprinkling a little cold water on the top to settle them, and adding a small pinch of salt.

Then she lit the stove and put the pot on top to keep the coffee warm. Hamish shaved and showered. In the kitchen, he gulped down two cups of black coffee. To Josie's dismay, he didn't seem to notice the difference from his usual brew.

Hamish had in fact noticed the difference and had seen the packet of real coffee but did not want to thank Josie in case she was encouraged to encroach on his home.

Before he left the station he phoned Jimmy, who told him that Hamish had the job of breaking the news to Mrs. Lussie.

"We're off to see Mark's mother," said Hamish as they drove off. "What was that boy up to? Some way he put himself in danger by not telling us all he knew. Either that or he suddenly remembered something. Did he phone his killer and make an appointment? I wonder if he had a mobile phone. I hope we can find something to narrow the suspects down. I hate this sort of job—breaking bad news."

But when they arrived at Mark's home, it was obvious the news had already been broken by the highland bush telegraph. Neighbours were crowded into a small living room, murmuring condolences as Mrs. Lussie sat and wept.

"I would like a word with Mrs. Lussie," said Hamish. "Will you all please wait outside?"

A large woman protested. "Cannae ye leave the wumman alone?" she cried.

But Mrs. Lussie rallied. She dried her eyes and said, "I'll speak to the sergeant. I want to find out who killed my boy."

"Now, Mrs. Lussie," said Hamish. "Did you hear Mark go out last night?"

She shook her head. "The baby was quiet for once so I got the first good sleep I've had in ages."

"Did he say anything at all that might be significant? Or did he look excited in any way?"

She dabbed at her eyes with an already sodden handkerchief. "He didn't say anything. He was reading a fillum magazine. Then we watched a bit o' telly and he said he was tired and wanted an early night."

"Did he have a mobile phone?"

"Yes, but he didn't use it much. Poor lost soul. He didn't seem to have that much friends. When we was with the church, he knew some young people, but he gave up the church."

"May we see his room?"

"It's up the stairs, first left."

As Hamish and Josie went up the stairs, the neighbours who had been watching through the front window crowded in again.

The room was unexpectedly neat for a young man's. It was quite small. There was a narrow bed, neatly made up, with a bedside table and reading lamp. A desk by the window with a hard upright chair in front of it held a pile of comics and film magazines. There was no computer or posters or pictures on the walls, which were covered in an oatmeal patterned wallpaper. A tall, thin wardrobe fronted by a long glass mirror stood against one wall, and a chest of drawers against another.

Hamish put on gloves and so did Josie. "You search the bedside table," he said, "and I'll have a look in the wardrobe."

There were few clothes hanging up: one dark blue suit and black coat, three long-sleeved shirts, a puffa jacket, and a tweed jacket. Underneath the clothes was a pair of black shoes and three pairs of sneakers. He searched in all the pockets but did not find anything. He even ran his gloved fingers along the insides of all the footwear in case anything had been hidden there.

"I've got his bank book and phone bill," said Josie.

Hamish took them from her. Mark had had a post office savings account with fifty pounds in it. The phone bill only

listed five numbers. One was to his home; Hamish's sharp eyes
had taken a note of the phone number on the receiver dial when
he had been downstairs. The other four were to a Strathbane
number. Hamish thought they would probably turn out to be
made to the wildlife park. He took out his mobile, dialled directory enquiries, asked for William Freemont's phone number, and gave the address of the wildlife park. The operator
gave him the number. It was the same number as the four on
the phone bill.

"Bag them up," he said to Josie. "That's the old phone bill.
We'll need to get Strathbane to check with the phone company
and find out if he phoned anyone last night. I'll just look in the
chest of drawers."

The top drawer contained underwear, the second socks, and
the third T-shirts. In the bottom drawer, there was a small
photo album and a selection of soft porn magazines. Hamish
flipped open the photo album. It contained pictures of Annie:
Annie as the Lammas queen, Annie at various church func-
tions, and a few of Annie taken when she was leaving her home.
Apart from the ones of Annie, there were no family pictures.

"Bag that as well," said Hamish, handing her the album.
"I'm just going to move this chest of drawers in case something's fallen down the back."

There was no carpet on the floor, only a sort of spongy li-
noleum. He heaved the chest of drawers away from the wall.
"What's this?" he exclaimed. He stretched down and brought
up a chemistry set. He sat down on the bed and carefully
opened it. Most of the chemicals had been used.

"That's it!" said Josie, leaning over him. "He was the bomber!"

"I think this is too basic to make such a sophisticated bomb," said Hamish. "It's probably just an old Christmas present."

"But there are no other toys or presents in the room," said Josie. "I mean, you'd think he would have old schoolbooks, or stuffed toys, or model airplanes, or something like that."

"We'll bag it up and take it. Let's see Mrs. Lussie again. It means getting rid of the neighbours."

Once more, Mrs. Lussie's sympathisers were told to wait outside. "We found a chemistry set in Mark's room," said Hamish. "When did he get that?"

"That was a while ago. A gentleman friend of mine gave it to him. He played with it for a bit and then forgot about it."

"We're taking it and some other things," said Hamish. "Mark didn't seem to keep anything much in his room. I thought we would find old toys or something like that."

"It was the church. They were collecting toys for the poor. Mark was told it was his Christian duty to bring everything in."

Hamish scribbled out a receipt and handed it to her. "Mrs. Lussie, if you can think of anything at all, please call me at the station in Lochdubh."

"When can I bury my son?"

"I'll tell the procurator fiscal to get in touch with you. They'll be calling soon anyway. I'm afraid they will want you to identify the body. Is there no relative who could do the identification instead? Where is your husband?"

"I don't know. He ran off after Mark was born."

"Name?"

"Sam Lussie."

"What did he do for a living?"

"Nothing much," she said bleakly. "He was on the dole."

"Is there anyone who could identify the body other than yourself?"

"I'll do it," she said tearfully. "I want a last look at my son."

Outside, Hamish phoned Jimmy. He said he was sending Police Sergeant Southern to collect Mrs. Lussie and take her to the procurator fiscal's office. Hamish told him about finding the chemistry set but added that it looked like too amateur a kit to have made the bomb. Jimmy said he was still up at the war memorial and if Hamish brought the chemistry set up to him, he would take it over to the forensic lab in Lochdubh. They would start by checking with the phone company as well.

The wind was screaming around the war memorial when they arrived. Above them, the black bronze statue of a Boer War soldier stared out across Braikie to the heaving sea.

"Can't find a thing what with this heather all about," complained Jimmy. "Oh, here comes our lord and master. Afternoon, sir, has Roger said anything yet?"

"Not a thing," said Blair, lumbering up to them, the cold wind raising red patches on his groggy face. "What have ye got?"

"Macbeth's just found a chemistry set in Mark Lussie's room," said Jimmy.

Blair visibly brightened. "That's it. Case closed."

"Not really, sir. The chemistry set looks like a kid's one. And we've still got to find out who murdered Mark."

"You," said Blair in a sudden fury, glaring at Hamish, "take your wee sidekick and get down there to thae houses and see if anyone saw anything."

Hamish repressed a sigh. As he looked down the hill, he could see police officers going door to door, but he said meekly, "Yes, sir."

He walked down the hill to where his Land Rover was parked. "Get in," he said to Josie.

"Aren't we going to . . . ?"

"No. Waste of time. That ground's being covered. We're going back to Lochdubh. I've got to think."

Once back at the police station, Josie followed him quietly in, not wanting him to be too aware of her presence and send her away.

Hamish went straight to the police office. Josie was glad the dog and cat were nowhere around. They came and went by a large cat flap on the kitchen door. Hamish sat down at his desk, and Josie pulled a chair up next to him.

"What I want to do," said Hamish, taking a notebook out of his desk, "is to make a list of all the suspects, and then we start somehow to check up and see if there is anything in any of their backgrounds to show they had the knowledge to make a bomb."

"Shall I make some coffee, sir?" asked Josie.

"Yes, that would be grand."

Josie went happily off to the kitchen where she was soon lost in a rosy dream of being Hamish's wife.

When she came back with two mugs of coffee and a plate of biscuits, Hamish was checking down a list he had made.

"I can't leave out Jake Cullen," he said. "I know he's dead but he might have murdered her before that. Maybe Annie knew something about drugs at that club and had threatened to tell the police. Now, I can't forget Bill Freemont."

"He seemed a stupid man," said Josie.

"He could have got someone to do it for him. I wonder if he has any criminal connections? Or Jocasta, his wife? No, scrub that one. I should think she's been too out o' love wi' him for a while to get jealous enough."

"Is your coffee all right?" asked Josie.

"Yes, chust fine. Don't sit so close to me. You're crowding me."

Josie blushed and drew her chair back.

"Then there's Jessie Cormack. Annie took her boyfriend away—and that boyfriend, Percy Stane, had better be on the list as well. I may as well put the minister, Mr. Tallent, down as well. I'll swear he was in love with Annie.

"But right at the moment, my main suspect is Barry Fitz-cameron. He's the spider in the middle o' the web."

The phone rang. It was Jimmy. "You'll never believe this, Hamish. Blair went up the brae a bit for a nip o' whisky out o' his flask. A great gust o' wind caught him and sent him tumbling down the brae right onto the crime scene and he banged his head on the plinth o' the memorial and went out cold. Daviot's here and he's furious. Blair's been taken to Braikie hospital."

"Hang on a minute, Jimmy." Hamish turned to Josie. "You

may as well take the rest of the day off, what's left of it. Run along."

He waited until Josie had left and then spoke urgently. "Jimmy, raid that disco tomorrow."

"You mean . . . ?"

"I don't want to think Blair was the informant, but do you think you could do it?"

"I'll tell Daviot I've had a tip-off."

"Just make sure Daviot doesn't go visiting Blair!"

"I'll tell him he's not allowed visitors for the next forty-eight hours."

Mrs. Wellington greeted Josie. "I've a nice venison casserole. You can have some of that. Sit down at the table. How's Hamish?"

"As usual," said Josie. "I'm thinking of getting a transfer back to Strathbane."

Mrs. Wellington was alarmed. The money she received for housing Josie had come in very handy.

"You haven't been having much fun here," she said. "You should go to the dance in the hall this Saturday."

"I don't want to go on my own," said Josie.

"Get Hamish to take you. That man needs a good woman."

"He won't want to go," said Josie.

"Oh, he will," said Mrs. Wellington. "I'll make him."

Mrs. Wellington thought that a nice clean girl like Josie McSween was just the kind to sort Hamish Macbeth out. That evening, her eyes gleaming with matchmaking, she made her way along to the police station.

"Come ben," said Hamish reluctantly.

Mrs. Wellington followed Hamish into his living room and looked around in disapproval. There were two dirty coffee mugs beside his armchair and sheets of notes spread out on the floor. The dog and cat lay sleeping in front of a smoky peat fire.

Yes, Josie was just what this lazy policeman needed in his life. "I want you to take Josie to the dance on Saturday," boomed Mrs. Wellington.

"I'm following up more than one murder," protested Hamish. "And it iss not the thing at all to be socialising with my policewoman."

Mrs. Wellington sank down in the little-used armchair opposite Hamish, sending up a cloud of dust.

"You must make an exception," she said. "That young girl has had no social life at all since she came here. One evening won't hurt you."

"But—"

"No buts, young man. I expect to see you there. There's been talk in the village about how lonely Josie must feel."

Hamish suddenly just wanted to get rid of her. "Oh, all right," he said ungraciously.

Josie was elated at the news. She escaped to her room and poured herself a large glass of whisky to celebrate. But then she began to wonder what would happen if Hamish Macbeth either did not dance or danced with her only once and then disappeared back to his station.

She drank more whisky and wondered what to do. She felt

she wouldn't get any sleep that night. Then she remembered that hidden in her luggage, she had a packet of Mandrax tablets. They had been part of a drug raid when she was in Strathbane. She had not been on the drug raid but had been given various drugs and told by Jimmy to take them down to the evidence lockers. It was only when she returned that she had found the packet in her pocket. Not wanting to get into trouble, she had taken them home with her. The missing tablets had not been noticed during the court case.

Mandrax, known as quaaludes in the States, was a banned drug. It was a powerfully addictive sleeping pill with dangerous side effects. Now, if she ground down some of the tablets and slipped it into Hamish's drink, he would start to get dizzy. She could help him back to the police station, get him into bed after undressing him, and then undress herself and climb into bed with him. When he woke up, she could say they had had sex. He would feel obliged to marry her.

The mad idea fuelled by more whisky began to seem perfectly feasible.

Hamish was awakened two mornings later by the ringing of the telephone. He struggled out of bed, glancing at the clock in alarm, realising he had slept in, and rushed to answer it. It was Jimmy. "Och, man," he said. "You'll never believe what's happened."

"What?"

"Roger Burton's escaped, but before he did he got into Barry's cell and killed him."

"How the hell did that happen?"

"Roger knocked out the copper who took him his breakfast. He dressed himself in the copper's clothes, put his own clothes on the policeman, and put the policeman in the bed in the cell wi' a blanket over him. He took his keys and found Barry's cell. He stabbed him to death."

"What with?"

"A sharpened toothbrush."

"What on earth was left in his cell to sharpen the damn thing?"

"Didn't need a knife. There's rough concrete on that ledge by the window. He just rubbed it and rubbed it down to a point."

"So you'd arrested Barry?"

"Aye, I forgot to tell you. We'd raided thon disco yesterday and found the stash o' drugs. Oh, God, we're all in deep crap here, right up to our oxters. Daviot is screaming blue murder and says if Blair had been around it wouldnae have happened. I tried to say that maybe we'd got Barry because Blair wasn't around and Daviot says I cannot defend myself by libelling a good officer."

"Any clue as to where Roger Burton is?"

"By the time they found out the fellow in the bed wasn't Roger, he'd long gone."

"What about the barman at the disco? He must know something."

"It gets worse. He was bailed and now he's disappeared as well. You're on your own wi' that valentine case. Getting anywhere?"

"Not so far. I've interviewed all my suspects again."

"Keep at it. Daviot's rampaging around. The duty officer's

been suspended, poor bastard, although it had nothing to do with him. We've got the press baying outside for blood and Daviot baying inside."

When Hamish rang off, he thought that Blair must be thrilled to bits. If there was a connection to Barry, it would be hard to find it now.

There was a knock at the kitchen door. He opened it. Josie stood there, smiling up at him.

"I'm late," said Hamish. "I was interviewing people until late last night."

"You should have let me help you, sir," said Josie.

"Get the coffee on and I'll be ready in a minute."

When Hamish finally appeared, dressed and shaved, Josie said, "It's kind of you to offer to take me to the dance tomorrow."

"I didn't offer," said Hamish, helping himself to coffee. "I was bullied into it."

He waited for Josie to say something like, *Oh, well, in that case, I'll go myself,* but she merely hung her head and looked miserable.

Hamish was suddenly sorry for her. "Don't worry, Josie," he said. "We'll probably have a good time."

He'd called her Josie! All Josie's dreams flooded into her brain. But she said, "Where are we going today?"

"I want to try to get Jocasta on her own. If I'm right, she's fed up with the marriage and might talk a bit freely if we can get her without her husband around."

*   *   *

The first thing they saw as they drove up to the wildlife park was a large FOR SALE sign. "Now, that is very interesting," said Hamish. "The marriage must be breaking up. Bill would never have let her sell."

He drove down the muddy slope to the office.

Jocasta was found poring over accounts books. "Oh, it's you," she said curtly. "Find a chair. I'll be with you in a minute."

They sat waiting patiently while Jocasta turned pages, muttering, "Bastard!" and "Unbelievable."

At last she sat back in her chair and said, "What?"

"Where is your husband?" asked Hamish.

"I neither know nor care. I'm filing for divorce. Bill ripping me off is one thing, but Annie Fleming was raiding the petty cash."

"You're sure of that?"

"Quite sure."

"And you really don't know where your husband is?" said Josie.

"No. We had a row. I said I was filing for divorce and he took off after I said I was selling the place. This folly is fortunately in my name. I told him I was going to sell the place to a builder. You should have seen his face! The idiot considers himself an environmentalist. Oh, he'll catch some other poor woman the way he caught me. I met him at one of those save-the-planet get-togethers in Edinburgh and he courted me and as soon as we were married, he sweet-talked me into this piece of rubbish. I used to be concerned about things like my carbon footprint. Now I don't give a damn if it's a carbon hobnailed boot. I want out."

"It is very hard to get building permission," said Hamish.

"I've got a loophole. I got building permission for this ratty office and the house and believe me that's going to cover a multitude of sins, meaning a few rows of nasty little bungalows."

"Have any of the creatures been returned to you?"

"Not a one. They were all, apart from the minks and the lion, from the local countryside. They're all probably happy in their natural habitat. And they hadn't been in the cages long enough to get used to being fed."

"Have any of the animal libbers been caught?"

She gave a cynical laugh. "No. I think you lot have enough on your hands what with an escaped hit man and a murder in the cells to bother about a few idiots."

"What did you think of Annie Fleming?" asked Hamish.

"A right little tart she turned out to be. I suspected there was something going on with Bill. I don't think she could leave anything in trousers alone."

"What about a kilt?" asked Josie seriously.

Hamish burst out laughing and Josie blushed. But Jocasta said, "About a month ago, I was walking out to the cages when I saw her up on the main road beside a four-by-four talking to a man in a kilt. He was all dressed up in the full rig like men wear when they're going to a wedding or an official function."

"What did he look like?"

"He was too far away. Medium height, dark hair. They saw me watching and he jumped in his vehicle and drove off.

"Then there was a weedy-looking youth hanging around. He kept trying to speak to Annie but she told him to get lost. I think she called him Percy."

"I know who you mean," said Hamish. "I think we'll be having a wee word with that young man again."

Back at the Land Rover, Hamish phoned police headquarters and asked for Mark Lussie's mobile phone number. He waited patiently until he got it. Then he said to Josie, "Before we go and see Percy again, I've got an idea. Maybe Mark's murderer threw that phone away in the heather."

Josie shivered as she bent before the wind and followed Hamish up the brae to the war memorial. Out to sea, dark clouds were massing, and she hoped Hamish would either find the phone or give up before the threatening rain arrived.

Hamish took out his own phone and dialled Mark's number. He began to walk away from the war memorial down the sloping hill on the other side. At the bottom of the hill was a small grocery shop with rubbish bins parked at the back.

"I wouldnae be surprised if he didnae dump the phone in one o' thae bins," he said.

"But the bins would have been cleared by now," said Josie.

"Aye, and that's why we're going to the council tip."

They reached the Land Rover just as the rain came down in sheets. "I haven't got a raincoat with me," said Josie.

"Did you bring your coveralls?" asked Hamish, meaning the plastic suit police wore at a crime scene so that they would not contaminate it.

"Yes, I got them."

"They'll do. Suit up when we get to the tip."

The tip was down at the end of a long lane leading to the sea between Lochdubh and Strathbane. Josie's heart sank when she saw the acres of rubbish stretched out under a stormy sky full of screeching, diving seagulls.

Hamish went into the office wearing black oilskins. He asked about the rubbish from the grocery and if the man in charge had any idea which part of the acreage it would end up in.

The man said vaguely it might be over to the far left of the dump.

With Josie trailing miserably behind, Hamish went over to the left, took out his phone, and dialled Mark's number.

The wind dropped and he swore he could hear a faint ringing sound. "Come on, Josie," he urged. "I think there's something here under this pile o' garbage."

That use of her first name spurred Josie into action. "I won't dial any more until we've dug down a bit," said Hamish.

He paused occasionally to admire Josie's diligence. He had been too hard on the lassie, he thought. After they had searched down a certain depth, he dialled again. "Hear that!" he cried triumphantly. He scrabbled down to the ringing sound, tossing filthy rubbish over his shoulder.

"Got it!" he cried at last. "Let's get back into shelter. This is grand." He seized hold of Josie and waltzed her round on top of the garbage.

Josie walked back to the Land Rover as if she were walking on air. "We'll get back to Lochdubh, dry out, and I'll get you something to eat," said Hamish once they were in shelter again. "Let me check this phone. What was the last call he made? Here, write this down."

Josie took out her notebook and wrote down the number

"Right," said Hamish. "Give it to me. Let's phone up and see who's at the other end."

He dialled and waited. A clear highland voice came on the line. "Town hall, Braikie," said the voice. "Which department?"

Hamish rang off, his hazel eyes gleaming. "That was the town hall. Maybe young Percy is deeper in this than I thought." He bagged Mark's mobile and stripped off his pair of latex gloves.

"I'm afraid we'd better take this over to Strathbane first. I'll blast the heater and dry us out."

Jimmy was just about to go out when they arrived. He wrinkled his nose. "You pair smell like hell."

Hamish held up the evidence bag. "We've found Mark Lussie's mobile at the council tip. The last call he made was to the town hall. So we're going to grab at bit to eat and get over there. How are you getting on?"

"I've barely started," complained Jimmy. "Questions and questions from the big yins up to interrogate us all about how we managed to let one murder happen and one dangerous killer escape. Barry's no loss."

"Who inherits his money?" asked Hamish.

"Probably the state will take most of it like they always do when someone has been profiting from drugs. His only living relative is his sister, a churchy woman, who's horrified at her brother's criminal activities. Got to go. Give me that phone and I'll get it over to forensics."

*   *   *

Hamish and Josie drove to a restaurant in Strathbane. A woman at the next table said loudly, "The day when policemen actually took a bath seems to be long over."

Josie dissolved into giggles.

"We really must smell something awful," said Hamish. "After this, we'll get back to Lochdubh and clean up. I've got an old uniform I can use. What about you?"

"I've got a spare recently," said Josie.

They had a pleasant meal. Hamish was in high good humour. He felt the case was beginning to break at last.

Josie thought about her mad dream of drugging him. What a silly idea!

At the town hall, Hamish asked to be directed to wherever the switchboard was. He was grateful that the town hall was old-fashioned and didn't go in for a phone tree—press one for so-and-so, press two for someone else, and so on.

The young girl at the switchboard seemed vaguely familiar. "Police," he said. "Just a few questions. What is your name?"

"Iona Sinclair."

"Have we met? I am Police Constable Hamish Macbeth."

"I saw you last year at the crowning of the Lammas queen. It was promised to me because Annie had been queen the year before, but she got it again which wasn't fair."

Iona was a tall girl in her late teens with hair as red as Hamish's own, green eyes, and freckled skin. She had the lilting accent of the Outer Hebrides.

"We're interested in a call that came through here to the

switchboard on the evening Mark Lussie was murdered," said Hamish.

"Well, we close at five o'clock. There were a lot of calls before then. People ask for various departments."

"Did anyone ask for waste disposal?"

"We get a lot of those. People are always girning on about the evil dustmen, persecuting them because the waste isn't in the proper bins."

"Did you know Annie Fleming well?"

"I was at school with her, but she wasn't popular with the girls. She was too busy chatting up the teachers."

"Anyone in particular?"

"Harry Massie, the English teacher."

"Is he still teaching at the school?"

"Last I heard."

Outside the town hall, Hamish sighed. "Another suspect. Let's see this English teacher."

"What about Iona?" asked Josie. "She must have borne a grudge against Annie."

"I haven't forgotten her," said Hamish. "But she doesnae seem the type to know how to put together a sophisticated bomb."

Harry Massie was a tall, rangy man in his late thirties. He had thick brown hair, a beaky nose, and a small mouth. He was wearing corduroy trousers and a well-worn Harris tweed jacket over a checked shirt open at the neck.

"We want to ask you about Annie Fleming," said Hamish.

Josie got an inner glow. Hamish was beginning to say *we*.

"Poor girl. Any idea who did it?"

"Not as yet. I must ask you this: Did Annie Fleming make a pass at you?"

"By all that's holy, someone who doesn't think she was a saint. Yes, she did."

"Explain what happened."

The classroom smelled of chalk, sweat, and dust. Outside the wind howled and screeched.

Harry leaned on his desk. "Annie was very good at English. Then she started waiting in the classroom until the others had left, asking me questions. I began to feel uneasy because other members of the staff began to tease me about being seen alone with Annie. So I told her that if she had any questions, to put them in writing and leave them on my desk and not to stay behind in the classroom. I was very firm with her. I held the door open for her and she . . . she stuck her tongue in my ear.

"I told her I would report her and she laughed and said who would ever believe me and if I didn't keep my mouth shut she would report *me* for having tried to rape her. I felt nothing but relief when she left the school for good."

"Who's the chemistry teacher here?"

"Sol Queen. But I hardly think . . ."

"Where can we find him?" asked Hamish.

Harry glanced at his watch. "He'll be in the staff room having a break. I'll take you along."

Various teachers were standing at an open window in the staff room, smoking and braving the gale that was blowing in.

"Sol," said Harry. "The police want a word with you."

An elderly teacher turned around. He had sparse grey hair and thick glasses. "We can't talk here," he said. "Come outside."

Josie and Hamish followed him into the corridor. "What is it?" he asked, peering myopically up at Hamish. Hamish thought that Annie could hardly have made a pass at this elderly gentleman, so he asked instead, "Is there anyone you can think of who might have the expertise to make a letter bomb?"

"Funnily enough, I've thought of that. But I cannot think of anyone at all—apart from me. I mean, I would know which chemicals to use, but I would not know how to install the fuse. That takes a lot of sophisticated knowledge."

Hamish had a sudden idea. "Do you have computer classes in the school?"

"No. We were supposed to get them, but there is so much else needing to be done here. The roof's in need of repair and it would mean finding extra money over the cost of the computers to hire another teacher."

Hamish thanked him and then, as they walked towards the entrance, he phoned Jimmy. "Did forensics go through Annie's computer?"

"She didnae have one," said Jimmy. "Her father says that computers are the instruments o' the devil. They searched the one at the wildlife place but nothing but business on it."

Hamish rang off. "I can't think of any young person who didn't use the Internet," he said. "There's that new Internet café, just off the main street. Let's try there."

✳   ✳   ✳

The Internet café was run by a Pole, Lech Nowak, and the place was full of Polish accents as other immigrants e-mailed home.

Hamish asked whether Annie Fleming had ever used the café. "The girl that was murdered? No, she never came in here," said Lech.

Another possible lead gone, thought Hamish gloomily.

The café sold snacks, so Hamish suggested they should both eat something. He hoped his pets were all right back at the police station. He was worried that the hit man might call back to finish the job and shoot the animals.

After they had finished eating, Hamish said, "I'm going back to that minister's. I know the parents have probably been interrogated but I want to speak to them myself. But I would like you to go back to the town hall and have a talk with Percy Stane. Make a friend of him. Sympathise. See if you can get anything more out of him and in a roundabout way, see if he got any phone calls from Mark."

Hamish was not looking forward to interviewing the Flemings. What sort of parents had produced such a manipulative drug-taking daughter?

Chapter Seven

☠

In for a penny, in for a pound—
It's Love that makes the world go round!

—W. S. Gilbert

Josie didn't get much out of Percy. He protested that he had never even met Mark Lussie, nor had he received any phone call. Josie tried to trick him by lying and saying she knew he had received a call from Mark Lussie, whereupon the usually rabbit-like Percy had rallied, telling her that she was lying and he would put in an immediate complaint about police harassment. Alarmed, Josie protested that perhaps she had received false information, but Percy simply held the office door open for her and told her to go.

The early northern night had fallen, and the wind whipped clouds across a cold little moon overhead.

Josie suddenly had an idea. She would get a taxi, go back to Lochdubh, clean up the police station, and have a hot supper waiting for Hamish when he returned.

✳   ✳   ✳

Hamish, meanwhile, was facing Mr. and Mrs. Fleming. He had expected to confront a pair of parental tyrants but found Annie's mother and father to be decent, ordinary, and grief-stricken.

"I believe, if you don't mind my saying so," said Hamish, "that you appear to have been rather strict with your daughter."

"We only did it for her own good," said Mr. Fleming. "She never protested. She was a good girl. I won't believe all those nasty stories that folk are circulating about her."

"Annie did have drugs on her body," said Hamish.

"Someone must have tricked her. We brought her up to fear the Lord and do the right thing."

Hamish turned his attention to Mrs. Fleming. She was in her late fifties, and he judged she must have had a baby later in life than most mothers. Her face had the drained, exhausted look of someone who has been crying for days.

"Mrs. Fleming," asked Hamish, "do you know of any particular friends she might have had?"

"No, she didn't socialise much with the young people from the church. She seemed happier with our friends when we had them round for tea." Hamish guessed that *tea* meant high tea, still served in the north in a lot of households instead of dinner.

"May I have the names of your friends?"

"Well, there's the Baxters."

"That would be your neighbours—Cora and Jamie Baxter?"

"That's right. And also old Mrs. McGirty. Mr. and Mrs. Tallent, of course. We all got on very well and Annie appeared to enjoy their company."

"The minister seemed to have been fond of Annie."

"He was so good. He pointed out the dangers a young person in this day and age could be subjected to. He even gave Annie private religious instruction."

"How often?"

"Sometimes twice a week in the evenings."

"And did this go on until her death?"

"No. Mr. Tallent said he had to give up the instruction because of the weight of parish duties."

Hamish made notes and asked several more questions. Then he asked, "Is Mr. Tallent at home?"

"I believe he is at the church," said Mr. Fleming.

Hamish walked to the low stone church next door. He opened the door and went in. It was a small kirk with pine pews and a stone-flagged floor. It was very cold. He remembered hearing that this was one of the stricter churches. It did not have an organ but made do with a chanter, a man who struck a tuning fork against one of the pews to introduce the hymn singing. He saw the huddled figure of the minister in a front pew. He was seated with his head buried in his hands.

Hamish went up to him. Although Mr. Tallent must have heard the sound Hamish's boots made on the stone floor, he did not move.

Hamish laid a hand on his shoulder and said quietly, "I need to be having another word with you, Minister. It's about that private religious instruction you were giving Annie."

Mr. Tallent raised his head. "I tried to protect Annie from this sinful world but she must have been corrupted by that creature Jake."

"I think Annie was quite good at corrupting people herself. Did she come on to you?" asked Hamish.

"What a disgusting suggestion!" raged the minister.

Hamish sat down beside him in the pew. "Look here," he said gently, "Annie was verra manipulative and she liked power. I think she made you fall in love with her. I think your conscience got the better o' ye and you stopped the lessons."

"She confessed to an admiration for me," said Mr. Tallent after a long silence. "I was sinfully flattered. I became impatient with my wife. I nearly lost my faith. Yes, I stopped the classes and said I would only see her in the kirk. She shrugged. Then she laughed at me and called me a silly old goat." Tears began to run unchecked down his cheeks. "I went a bit mad. I even thought of killing her. But I didn't. Believe me, Sergeant, I wouldn't know how to begin to make a letter bomb.

"Does any of this have to come out? It would devastate my wife and daughter. And the scandal!"

"Chust so long as I don't find any proof linking you with the murder, I'll keep quiet," said Hamish, feeling embarrassed faced with the man's grief and shame.

When he got out of the Land Rover in front of the police station, he found Willie Lamont waiting for him with the dog and cat at his heels. Willie had once been a policeman, working for Hamish, but he had fallen in love and married the beautiful daughter of the owner of the Italian restaurant and had gone happily into the catering trade.

"What's up, Willie?" asked Hamish.

"Sonsie and Lugs were around the restaurant and I thought it was time to bring them hame."

"You know where the key is, Willie. You shouldnae be standing here in the cold."

"I don't know where the key is. I tried the door but it's locked. There's someone inside moving about and that big cat flap is jammed shut."

Hamish took out his own key and snapped open his baton. "Stand back, Willie," he said quietly.

He quietly unlocked the door. Josie was standing over the stove, wearing a frilly apron over a short black dress and high heels.

"What in God's name do you think you're playing at, McSween?" roared Hamish. He swung round and looked down at the cat flap. It had been taped shut. "And why are my poor beasties out in the cold?"

"I-I th-thought it would be great to take you a meal and give the place a bit of a clean," wailed Josie.

"Out!" shouted Hamish. "Get the hell oot o' here and neffer, effer do anything like this again. Shoo! Get lost."

Josie burst into tears. She seized her coat from a chair and ran out into the night.

"Wimmin," said Hamish, taking out a clasp knife and beginning to slice the tape on the cat flap.

"Och, you was awfy hard," said Willie. "The lassie meant well. Look how clean the place is."

"It's my home," said Hamish. "Thanks for looking after my beasts, Willie."

Willie left but Hamish was not to be left in peace for long. A wrathful Mrs. Wellington descended on him. "That poor girl is crying her eyes out, you brute. Instead of thanking her, all you did was shout at her."

"She had no right to just invade my home——"

"It's not a home. It's a police station."

"It iss my home. She shut my animals out in the cold."

"What you need is a decent woman in your life. You will take Josie to that dance tomorrow and behave like a gentleman."

Hamish refused to go to the manse with Mrs. Wellington and apologise. To Mrs. Wellington, Josie was the daughter she never had. She could not bear to see her so upset and so she lied and said that Hamish was really sorry and was looking forward to the dance.

When Josie went up to her room that night, she fished a bottle of whisky out from under her mattress and began to drink steadily. She had loved being in charge of the police station. She wanted to get married and never have to work as a policewoman again. As the whisky sank down the bottle, she came to a decision. She shook out tablets of Mandrax and, with the hilt of a knife, began to crush them into powder.

✻ ✻ ✻

Hamish decided to take the Saturday off. He hoped as he went around his property, seeing to his sheep and hens, and making some repairs, that his mind might clear. He had too many suspects, all whirling around his brain.

After lunch, he walked along to visit his friend Angela Brodie, the doctor's wife.

"Come in, Hamish," said Angela. "It's all round the village that your poor policewoman was just trying to give the place a bit of a cleanup and make you supper, and you shouted the place down."

"Angela, she locked my animals out in the cold. I'm investigating the murder of Annie Fleming who seems to ha' been one manipulative bitch and I don't want to have to deal with another one."

"Now, that's too harsh. She seems like a nice girl."

"Oh, well, maybe I did go a bit over the top. The truth is, I got a real fright. I'm always worried that Roger Burton, the hit man, might come back to finish the job. Could you be looking after Sonsie and Lugs while I'm at the dance?"

"Didn't you stop to think I might be going to the dance myself?"

"No, sorry."

"Okay. Just this once. As it happens, I'm not going. How's the murder investigation?"

"It's a right mess. Too many suspects. If ever a girl was just asking to be murdered by some man, it was Annie Fleming."

"Have a coffee and tell me all about it."

So in between sips of Angela's horrible coffee, Hamish outlined all that he had found out so far.

When he had finished, Angela said, "You're concentrating on the men. Have you considered the women? I mean, you'd expect a man to bash her over the head or strangle her. Making a letter bomb takes time and plotting and planning. Your murderer might be one very jealous woman. There was a lot of ill feeling when Annie was elected to be the Lammas queen two times running. She could have put someone's nose out of joint. To be Lammas queen means getting on TV and being interviewed and photographed in all the local papers. A lot of young people these days want instant fame without doing anything to get it. It's all the fault of reality TV."

"I'll think about it. But right now, Angela, my poor head can't bear the thought of any more suspects."

Hamish had phoned the manse and said that he would meet Josie at the dance. He dressed in casual clothes and, followed by Sonsie and Lugs, walked along to Angela's house.

"You're a bit late," said Angela.

"I'm reluctant," said Hamish. "I'll only go for a few dances and then clear off."

"Josie's quite pretty, you know."

"Maybe I'm being hard on her, but there's something awfy needy about her."

"Male vanity, Hamish. That's all it is. Now get along to that dance!"

Josie had refused all offers to dance. Her dreams of being held in Hamish's arms had been shattered. It was to be an evening of Scottish country dancing and the hall was loud with the drumming of feet and the hoochs of the dancers as they swung one another around. Josie felt overdressed. Nearly everyone was wearing casual clothes whereas she was dressed in a short skirt with a plunging sequinned blouse and very high heels.

At last, she saw Hamish's flaming-red head across the dance floor. Just as he came up to her, an Eightsome Reel was announced. "Shall we?" asked Hamish.

They joined a set and the band of fiddles, drums, and accordion struck up. Josie realised quickly the folly of wearing such high heels. She thought her ankles might break.

When the dance was over, Hamish said, "I could do with a drink. What about you?"

Josie picked up her evening bag from where she had left it and said eagerly, "That would be grand."

There were only soft drinks on offer. "Orange juice?" suggested Hamish.

"Yes, thank you." There was no barman. People just helped themselves. Hamish poured out two tumblers of orange juice and was about to hand one to Josie when Freda Campbell, the schoolteacher, came up just as a Strip the Willow was being announced. "Come on, you lazy copper," she said. "This is my dance."

"All right," said Hamish. "But where's your man?"

"Matthew's working late." Matthew was the editor of the *Highland Times.*

Josie watched as Hamish led Freda into the dance. Her eyes narrowed. She could have sworn Freda was flirting with him. She fished in her bag, took out the screw of paper containing the powdered Mandrax, and slipped it into one of the glasses of orange juice.

The energetic dance seemed to go on forever. Hamish crossed hands with Freda and danced down the line with Freda laughing up at him. Hamish may have been a lousy disco dancer but he was in his element when it came to Scottish country dancing.

At last it was over and Hamish and a big crowd approached the refreshment table. "Ah, orange juice. Just what I need," boomed Mrs. Wellington. To Josie's horror, she seized Hamish's doctored drink and gulped it down.

A Gay Gordons was announced. Hamish turned reluctantly to Josie, but Archie Maclean came up and whispered, "Outside, Hamish."

"Be back in a minute, Josie," said Hamish. He followed Archie outside, where men were gathered passing whisky around.

Hamish stood chatting and drinking until there appeared four youths, helping a dazed Mrs. Wellington from the hall. "She's come over faint," said one. "We're just going to run her up to the manse."

Josie appeared and said hurriedly, "I'd better go with her and make sure she's all right."

What if they called Dr. Brodie, worried Josie. He might suspect she had been drugged and order a blood test.

At the manse, Mrs. Wellington was heaved upstairs and laid on her bed. "I think I know what the matter must be," said the minister. "My wife sometimes takes a sleeping pill and she takes high blood pressure medicine as well. She must have mixed up her pills."

Josie felt a wave of relief. "If you think she'll be all right, I'll just go back to the dance."

But when she returned to the hall, it was to find that Hamish had left. "Where's Hamish gone?" Josie asked Archie Maclean.

"Och, when you werenae here, herself, Miss Halburton-Smythe, turned up and she and Hamish went off together."

Josie felt outraged. How dare he! But there was still time to put her plan into action. She had Mandrax pills left. If she let herself into the police station and doctored a glass of whisky and left it on the kitchen table, with any luck Hamish might have a nightcap. If by any chance Hamish and Priscilla were there, well, she had an excuse. She could say she was calling to find out why he had left the dance so early.

Hamish was seated in the bar of the Tommel Castle Hotel, looking gloomily at Priscilla.

"Why Australia?" he asked.

"I'm a computer programmer, Hamish," said Priscilla patiently. "The firm I was contracted to outsourced all the work to India and it's happening all over London. I've got a chance of this job in Sydney. I love Sydney."

"It's awfy far away," said Hamish miserably. "The hotel's doing great. It's not as if you have to work."

"Hamish, ever since Daddy lost all his money and we had to turn our home into this hotel, I've liked to make my own money just in case Daddy decides to play the stock market again. I'm lucky to get such a good job in the middle of a recession. Didn't you go to the dance with your policewoman?"

"I was bullied into it by Mrs. Wellington. I wish Josie McSween would just pack up and go back to Strathbane."

"Why? She seems a nice enough girl."

"There's something clingy about her and she's a rotten officer. She should never ha' joined the police force."

"So where are you in the case?"

"Nowhere—except for an idea of Angela's. I've been checking up on all the men in the case. She suggests it might have been some woman."

"I can see the wisdom of that. A jealous woman will go to any lengths."

"Could you put me up for the night, Priscilla? I've a feeling if I go back home, Josie will be waiting for me."

"I'll find you something."

Josie put the crushed tablets in a glass of whisky and placed it on the kitchen table. She stirred the contents with a spoon. Now, she thought, let's hope he drinks it. I'll come back around two in the morning and hope he's asleep. She thought it a rare bit of luck that Hamish's pets were away somewhere. She made her way back to the manse over the fields at the back so that no one would see her. At one point, she stopped and listened. She had an odd feeling of being watched. The night was still and cold. She hurried on, anxious to get to her room and to a bracing glass of whisky.

Roger Burton, crouched behind a dry-stone wall, watched her go. He had returned to finish the job of getting rid of Hamish. He felt his reputation was at stake. It had got around the criminal fraternity in Glasgow that the hard man, Roger, had been attacked by a cat.

Now he was primed and ready to kill not only Hamish but those wretched animals of his as well.

He eased his way down the back slope to the station. It was in darkness. He tried the door and then grinned. It was unlocked. He threw it open, rifle at the ready.

Silence.

He fumbled for the light and switched it on. He rapidly searched the small station. No Hamish. No animals.

He sat down at the kitchen table, facing the door, rifle at the ready. He saw the glass of whisky in front of him. Just the thing. He usually never drank until the job was over, but one wouldn't hurt. He drank it down, wrinkling his nose at the taste and wondering whether it was moonshine from one of the illegal stills he believed to be up in the hills.

Then Roger began to feel so very sleepy. The hallucinatory effect of the drug began to take over. He felt he was back in his own flat in East Glasgow. He stumbled through to the bedroom, stripped off his clothes, crawled into Hamish's bed, and fell asleep.

At two in the morning, Josie quietly made her way back to the police station. She frowned when she found the door unlocked. She should have remembered to lock it. She let herself in and switched on the light. The first thing she saw was the empty whisky glass on the table. Josie picked it up and scowled down at the remnants of white powder at the bottom of the glass. If

Hamish saw that, he'd get it analysed. She rinsed it out, dried it, and put it up on the shelf with the others.

Now for action!

She went quietly into the bedroom. Her foot struck something on the floor. She looked down and found herself staring at a rifle. She switched on the bedroom light. Josie did not recognise Roger although after the murder of Barry his photograph had been in all the papers and he was lying with his face half buried in the pillow. She only knew it was not Hamish and let out a gasp of dismay.

Josie ran from the police station as if the hounds of hell were after her.

In the morning, Angela stopped outside the police station and said to Sonsie and Lugs, "Off you go."

She watched until they had both disappeared through the large cat flap and then turned and walked away along the waterfront.

A sharp bark awoke Roger. He groggily struggled awake. The there was a menacing hiss. His startled eyes saw that damn cat staring at him, fur raised.

With a cry of terror, he leapt for the bed and straight for the kitchen door. The cat leapt on his back, digging her claws in. He howled and shook her off and, with blood running down his naked back, he fled along the waterfront to the alarm and amazement of the villagers out doing their morning shopping.

Nessie Currie was just about to get into her old Ford when a naked Roger dragged her from the car and dumped her on the road. Then he drove off, leaving her screaming.

*   *   *

Hamish was enjoying a leisurely breakfast at the hotel when he heard the news. He jumped in the Land Rover and set off in pursuit. He called Strathbane for backup. Roadblocks were hurriedly set up. All day long the search went on but Roger appeared to have disappeared into thin air.

How on earth could a bloody naked man just vanish?

It was only by evening when Nessie was coherent enough to be interviewed and the sedative Dr. Brodie had given her had worn off that she revealed she had been about to take a bundle of secondhand clothes from the village to a charity shop in Strathbane. When the report then came in from a man outside Inverness that a large woman had stolen his van, they realised that Roger had stopped to put on women's clothes and a big felt hat, formerly the property of Mrs. Wellington. The van had a full tank of petrol and two spare tanks in the back. Nessie's car was found dumped in a back street in Inverness.

The story was in all the newspapers the next morning. The comic side of it was fully exposed.

Here was a dreaded hit man who had gone to sleep in a police station, been attacked by a cat, run through the village naked, and escaped dressed as a woman.

Only Josie knew what had happened. She thanked her stars she had been wearing gloves when she had left the whisky.

Roger sat in his dingy flat and cursed his luck. Everything had been left behind: his false papers, false credit cards, mobile phone, and prized deer rifle, not to mention his car.

Two days later, he looked out of his window and saw a low

black Mercedes stopping outside his flat. His heart sank as he saw crime boss Big Shug climbing out of the car.

Roger shoved a pistol in the waistband of his trousers and went to open the door.

Big Shug looked like a prosperous Glasgow businessman from his well-tailored coat to his shining shoes.

"Been reading about me, have ye?" asked Roger. "Come in."

"I don't go much by what the papers say," said Big Shug. "But I've got a difficult job and I want you to off someone for me."

Roger said cautiously, "Are you sure the person you want to off isnae me?"

"Come on, laddie. When have I ever let you down? This is a delicate one. It's a woman. Anything against that?"

"Not a thing."

"Why did you kill Barry?"

"He would have talked and the drugs would have been traced right back to you."

"Aye, well, let's get going."

"Now?"

"No time like the present."

"Who is she?"

"Tell you when we get there."

Big Shug sat in the front with his driver and Roger sat in the back with one of his henchmen. No introductions were made. The Mercedes slid smoothly off.

"Where are we going?" asked Roger as the car began to drive along the Dumbarton dual carriageway.

"Relax, laddie. A wee bit before Helensburgh."

A thin mist was hovering over the Gairloch as the Mercedes

slid into a deserted building site. "Where is she?" asked Roger as he got out of the car.

"Along presently."

Big Shug whipped a gun out and shot Roger in the stomach. "That's one for Barry," he said. "He was a pal o' mine and he never would ha' talked."

He marched up to where Roger lay writhing on the ground and put two bullets into his head.

"Right, lads," he said. "Get to work. This site's held up forever waiting planning permission. Nobody'll be along here for ages."

His two henchmen dug a grave in the soft ground, dropped the body in, filled in the hole, and patted it flat with the backs of their spades.

They all got into the Mercedes and drove off.

Two little boys crouched behind a rickety wall of planks, having seen the whole thing. Rory Mackenzie was eight years old and his brother, Diarmuid, ten. "Do you think yon was real?" whispered Rory. "Maybe they was filming *Taggart*." He was referring to a popular Scottish television crime series.

"I think we'd better tell the police anyway." Diarmuid took out his much-prized mobile phone and dialled 999.

Chapter Eight

Love is like a dizziness,
It winna let a poor body
Gang about his bizziness.

—James Hogg

The murders of Mark Lussie and Annie Fleming had disappeared from the newspapers and from any of Strathbane's investigations. Hamish greeted the news of Roger Burton's murder with relief. It was Strathclyde's case, and, as he alone was still determined to solve the local murders, he was happy to let them get on with it.

Strathbane was a violent town, and the police were used to having unsolved murders on their books.

Josie begged leave to visit her mother, and Hamish let her go. Flora McSween welcomed her daughter and asked how her "romance" with Hamish was getting on.

Josie said that Hamish had taken her to a local dance, and Flora eagerly begged for details. Not wanting to disappoint her mother, Josie gave a highly embroidered account full of "speaking glances" and "warm clasped hands," which, to a less woolly-minded romantic than her mother, would have sounded like something out of the pages of a Victorian novel.

But as she talked, Josie's imagination, fuelled by a generous glass of whisky, began to make her lies become reality. Acute jealousy made her think of Priscilla as a rival, although she did not tell her mother that Hamish had gone off with Priscilla and had not returned until the following day.

Then Flora said, "I've been meaning to throw a lot of old stuff out of the attic. It's been up there for years and years. Some of it's even your Great-Great Aunt Polly's belongings. I know they're a part of family history but I thought some of the old clothes could go to the local dramatic society."

"I'll have a look tomorrow," said Josie.

On the following morning, Josie, nursing a hangover, climbed up to the attic, a small room at the top of the Victorian house which had once been used by a maid. Her mother followed her. "Look at all this stuff," said Flora. "What I want you to do, pet, is take a look through it and see if there's anything you want. I phoned the dramatic society and a couple are coming around this afternoon. I'll leave you to it."

Josie sat down and gloomily surveyed the jumble piled up around the room. Her mother had already labelled several of the old steamer trunks CLOTHES, PHOTOGRAPHS, and SHOES.

Feeling she could not really be bothered and wondering whether her mother had any Alka-Seltzer in the house, Josie decided to sit as long as she could, nursing her hangover, and then say there was nothing she wanted. She had no interest in family history. There were plenty of photographs downstairs of her late father whom she dimly remembered from her childhood as being an angry violent man, particularly on Friday evenings when he came back from the pub.

Her eyes fell on an old desk in the corner. It had a square wooden box on the top. Josie rose to her feet. Her mother had not said anything about jewellery. But perhaps there might be something valuable in there.

She opened the lid. It was full of old bottles of medicine and pillboxes. She was about to close the lid again when she noticed that one dark green bottle with a stoppered top had fallen on its side. It was labelled LAUDANUM. She lifted it out. It was full. She remembered reading in historical romances that laudanum was tincture of opium. She looked down into the jumble of medicines and found another bottle, also full.

After her failure to drug Hamish, she had vowed she would never, ever do anything so crazy again. But . . . maybe she would take them. You never knew . . .

Hamish meanwhile had set out to interview all the women in the case again. He was having a hard time with Cora Baxter, who seemed to think it the height of impertinence that a lowly police sergeant should dare to question a councillor's wife. Hamish first asked her if she had visited the town hall on the evening Mark Lussie was murdered and then asked her if she had, or if she knew anyone who had, a knowledge of chemistry.

Her formidable bosom heaved. "Are you daring to suggest

that *I* had anything to do with Annie's murder? I shall report you to your superiors."

"By all means," said Hamish, hoping she would do so and that his sergeant's stripes would be removed along with Josie. "I am simply—"

The door to the living room crashed open and Jamie Baxter strode in. "What's going on here?"

"Oh, Jamie," wailed Cora. "This terrible man is accusing me of murder!"

"This is too much, Macbeth," said Jamie. "Get out of here this minute and don't ever bother my poor wife again."

Hamish tried to protest that he was only doing his duty but he was firmly shown the door.

He trudged along to Mrs. McGirty's. As the frail old lady answered his knock, Hamish realised that she was the last person in the world to make a letter bomb, but maybe she heard useful gossip.

"Come in," said Mrs. McGirty. "I'll put the kettle on. Go into the living room and take a seat."

He was glad to see she had a real fire. He remembered his mother telling him that at one time when the Hydro Electric Board had started up, the Highlands were promised cheap electricity. Fireplaces were blocked up and electric fires placed in front of them: old oil lamps which now would fetch a good bit of money in some auction room were tossed out with the rubbish. The electricity turned out to be expensive but a lot of people kept the electric fires, the house-proud ladies of the Highlands claiming that peat and coal fires caused dust.

The small room was cluttered and cosy, the sofa and armchair being covered in paisley-patterned cotton slipcovers. There was a highland scene above the fireplace, darkened by years of smoke from the coal fire.

Mrs. McGirty came in carrying a laden tray. "Now there's tea and some of my scones, Mr. Macbeth. Help yourself."

Hamish did, realising he was hungry. When he had drunk two cups of tea and eaten two scones, in between times talking about the weather, he asked, "Have you heard any gossip in the town about anyone who might have wanted to murder Annie?"

"Too much gossip," said Mrs. McGirty, shaking her old head. "Quite terrible it is. Who would have thought that Annie Fleming was so bad? Folks have only just started telling me about her."

"The thing is," said Hamish, "thon letter bomb would have to have been made by someone with a knowledge of chemistry."

"Maybe not." The old lady's shrewd eyes looked up at him. "You can get all the information on stuff like that off the Internet these days."

"How do you know?"

"I looked it up myself. I have the computer. That way I keep in touch with the relatives in Canada."

"But where would anyone get the chemicals?"

"They're easily come by. Any schoolboy could probably pinch them out of the laboratory at school."

Hamish stared at her, his cup of tea halfway to his mouth. Sol Queen, the chemistry teacher, was too sane, too old, and too respectable. But what about a schoolboy? Annie had only really been interested in older men, except that she had wound up with Mark Lussie and Percy Stane.

He put his cup down in the saucer. "Did you see Bill Free-mont visiting Annie when her parents were out?"

"I saw his van outside and then after a bit I saw him come out of the house and get into it. I never thought one bad thing. I only thought it was nice of her boss to call on her when she was off sick."

"No one else?"

"Not that I know. But I spend a lot of time on the computer. It's the great thing for an old body like me."

"I have so many suspects my head's in a whirl," said Hamish. "But there was some phone call from Mark to the town hall before he died."

"Maybe the girl on the switchboard could help."

"Iona Sinclair? I'm afraid not. She gets so many calls asking to be put through to one department or another."

"I did hear there was a bit of a row over Annie being the Lammas queen two years running. Iona was bitter, folk are saying. But, och, it is terrible in the town with everyone hinting that it could be this one or that one."

"I forgot to ask Iona," said Hamish, "if there is someone who relieves her at the switchboard. I mean, what happens when she goes for lunch?"

"The town hall shuts between one and two."

"But say she wanted to go to the ladies' room?"

"You'll just need to ask."

*   *   *

When Hamish left her, he looked at his watch. It was just before one o'clock. He sped off to the town hall and parked outside.

He waited, hoping that Iona would emerge and not settle for sandwiches at her desk. When he saw her come out, he jumped down from the Land Rover and went to meet her.

"Iona! I would like to be having a wee word with you. What about lunch?"

"Wouldn't mind. I usually go to Jeannie's in the High Street." Jeannie's was a café run by a bad-tempered matron but popular because of the good quality of the snacks she served.

They both ordered Welsh rarebit and a pot of tea. "Now, Iona," began Hamish, "what happens when you have to leave the switchboard? Who relieves you?"

"Anyone who happens to be passing. Or I phone someone like, say, Jessie Cormack and ask her if she would mind taking over while I have a pee."

"So," said Hamish, "let's go back to the day Mark Lussie was murdered. Just before you closed for the evening, did anyone take over for you?"

She wrinkled her brow. Then her face cleared. "Oh, I mind fine. I was bursting and Mrs. Baxter was just coming out of her husband's office. So I called to her and asked if Jessie was very busy because I had to go to the loo and herself says, 'Run along. I'll do the board for you.'"

"You're sure about that?"

"'Course I'm sure. I'm hardly likely to forget Mrs. High and Mighty stooping to help someone like me out."

"But you didnae say anything about this when I first questioned you."

"You were asking me about calls I put through and it fair flustered me and I forgot about Mrs. Baxter."

"I heard you were bitter about Annie being made Lammas queen two years running," said Hamish.

"I was right furious. I went around swearing I'd kill the conniving bitch." Iona turned red. "I didn't, mind. I wouldn't. The provost, Mr. Tarry, got to hear about my complaints and he sent for me and told me if I wanted to keep my job, I'd better shut up. He said the council had voted unanimously for Annie. Annie flirted with anything in trousers. She probably went out of her way to make sure she'd be elected."

Hamish drove her back to the town hall and then braced himself to go and confront Cora again. To his relief, he saw that her husband's car was no longer outside the house.

The curtain twitched as he walked up the front path and rang the bell.

Cora answered the door, her well-upholstered bosom heaving with outrage. "You dare to come here again!"

"Now, now," said Hamish soothingly. "We may haff got off on the wrong foot. I haff chust learned that on the day Mark Lussie was murdered, you took over the switchboard for a wee while. I need to ask you about that for, you see, the last call Mark Lussie made was to the town hall."

She stared at him with those eyes of hers which were like Scottish pebbles and then said abruptly, "You'd better come in."

Hamish followed her back into the living room and removed his cap.

"Sit down," she barked.

Hamish sat down on a leather armchair, which welcomed him with the usual rude sound.

"Can you remember any calls?" he asked.

"Nothing in particular."

"It would have come from someone who sounded like Mark—a young person."

"There was a call to be put through to town planning—that was a woman—and one for health and safety—that was a man, not young—and one for waste disposal. The one for waste disposal sounded young. That's all I can remember."

Hamish took out his notebook and checked it. "Waste disposal. That would be Percy Stane."

"Yes, that's him."

"Did any of the callers ask for anyone by name?"

"No, just the department."

"Not many people would know how to operate an old-fashioned switchboard like the one at the town hall."

"I was a secretary at the town hall before I married my husband. I used to fill in on the switchboard. If you have no more questions, I may warn you," she said as Hamish headed for the door, "that my husband has already reported you to Superintendent Daviot."

"Oh, good," said Hamish, and he left her staring after him.

Hamish went to the town hall and walked into Percy Stane's office. Percy looked up at him, his eyes wide with fear like a trapped animal's.

"I've told you all I know," he blurted out.

"There might be something you have forgotten," said

Hamish. "Look, try to remember the day Mark Lussie died. Did you get a phone call?"

"I didn't know him all that well. I wouldn't know his voice."

Percy wrinkled his brow in thought. Then his face cleared. "There was the one call. When I said, 'Waste Disposal,' the voice said, 'Wrong department. Put me back to the switchboard.'"

"Man or woman?"

"A man. Maybe young. He didn't say which department he really wanted."

"Keep thinking about it and if you remember anything at all, here's my card. Give me a call. Do you know if the provost is in his office?"

"He'll be at the bank."

Hamish walked out to the main street and along to the West Highland Bank where Gareth Tarry, the provost, was the manager.

He was told to wait. Hamish waited and waited. He wondered whether the provost was really busy or simply one of those irritating people who like to show off their authority.

At last, he was ushered in. "I'm very busy, Sergeant," he said, "and I don't see how I can be of any help to you."

"How come Annie Fleming was elected Lammas queen two years running?"

"It was put to a vote. A secret ballot. There are ten councillors and all of them voted for Annie."

"That's odd, considering some of them hae daughters of their own."

"I can prove it! I still have the ballot papers."

"Where?" asked Hamish. "At the town hall?"

"No, in my safe here. Wait a moment. I just shoved the box in there. I'm more here than at the town hall and so I keep a lot of official stuff in the safe."

He rose, went to a large safe in a corner of his office, and fiddled with the combination. He bent down and scrabbled about on the inside, finally lifting out a square wooden box with a slot in the top. "I need the key," he muttered. He went to his desk and searched through the drawers, finally producing a small brass key.

He placed the box on his desk and unlocked it. "See for yourself."

Hamish took out several of the folded ballot papers and opened them. His eyebrows rose up to his hairline in surprise. "These are all typed! That's odd. You'd think they'd just scribble a name. Why go to the bother of typing it? Did you vote?"

"No, I never vote unless a casting vote is needed."

"Weren't the councillors surprised when you said the vote was unanimous?"

"I simply told them that Annie had been voted for."

"Who's the nearest councillor to here?"

"There's Garry Herriot. He runs the ironmonger."

Garry Herriot was a small, prim man dressed in a brown overall. He had very pale grey eyes.

"Mr. Herriot," Hamish began, "can you tell me who you voted for to be Lammas queen last year?"

"I voted for Iona, the lassie on the switchboard."

"Would it surprise you to learn that all ten votes were for Annie Fleming?"

"Yes, it would. I happen to know of two others who voted for Iona. What happened?"

"One of you got into that ballot box and put in a list of typed votes for Annie. Did you type yours?"

"No, I just wrote Iona's name on the slip of paper and popped it in the box. But the box was on the provost's desk and it was locked."

"Did the provost count out the votes in front of you all?"

"No, he just said Annie had been voted again. We all assumed she'd got the majority of votes."

"The provost can't be in the town hall all the time. He must spend most of the day at the bank."

"His secretary, Alice Menzies, handles all the phone calls and things like that."

Hamish went back to the town hall and got directions to Alice Menzies's room. He wondered whether Alice would turn out to be some other highland beauty whose nose had been put out of joint by Annie. But she turned out to be a middle-aged woman in a tweed suit and wearing thick spectacles. Hamish told her about the ballot papers.

"That's awful," she said. "But you can stop looking for the culprit. I know who did it."

At last, thought Hamish.

"It was Annie herself," said Alice. "She came up here just before the ballots were due to be counted. She said she had an appointment with Mr. Tarry. I told her to go along to the bank but she said the provost had told her to wait in the town hall office. I let her in. She was only there a short time and then she came out and said she must have made a mistake."

"Where is the key to the ballot box kept? I know the provost locked it up in the safe in the bank."

"You'll never believe this. The key was kept in a top drawer of his desk. Annie could have taken it out and unlocked the box."

"And didn't you think to report this when the vote was announced?"

She shrugged. "I was so used to all the men drooling over Annie, I didn't really bother about it."

"Why did Mr. Tarry take the ballot box to the bank?"

"It was right after the Lammas fair. His office was being decorated. He took a lot of files and the ballot box along to the bank."

"Were any of the councillors particularly interested in Annie?"

"I don't know. I mean, she didn't work here."

"What did Mr. Tarry say when you told him about her calling here for an interview?"

"It slipped my mind. The appointment wasn't down in the diary."

Hamish returned in the evening to his police station, feeling depressed. Josie was waiting for him outside.

"Have a good time in Perth?" asked Hamish.

"Yes, thank you. I wondered what we were going to do tomorrow."

Hamish thought quickly. He wanted rid of her. "Come in," he said. He led the way into the office and pointed to a large ordnance survey map on the wall. "I want you to take the As-synt Road between Lochinver and Kylesku. Drop off at each place and ask if everything is all right."

"Can't I help you with the murder enquiries?"

"It's large beat we have to cover. Leave the murder enquiries to me."

Josie set out the following morning in a sulky mood. But her spirits rose after she left Lochinver and set out on the As-synt Road along the coast. It was a rare calm, sunny day. The Minch lay placid with large glassy waves curling on the shore. She stopped at Drumbeg for a cup of tea and a sandwich, and then stood outside in the car park and breathed in the clear air. The majestic bulk of Quinag mountain rose up to a perfectly blue sky. The majesty of the Highlands seized her for the first time.

I belong here, she thought fiercely—me and Hamish Macbeth.

By the time she reached Kylesku by Loch a' Chairn Bhain and swept over the new road in the direction of Lairg, she was determined to do everything she could to capture Hamish.

It never entered her mind again that the way to Hamish's heart might be through some diligent police work. She had not asked at any of the villages along the coast if anyone had anything to report.

By the time early night had fallen, she pulled to the side of the road, her heart beating hard. She fished in her handbag for the half bottle of whisky she had bought earlier and sat drinking and dreaming. She had the two bottles of laudanum with her. When she returned to Lochdubh, if the police station was empty, she would doctor a glass of whisky. If Hamish arrived while she was in the police station, she would simply say that she had called to report on her day.

With a lurch in her stomach, she realised she had not talked to anyone in any of the villages. She could only hope Hamish would not ask for names.

Josie arrived back in Lochdubh at six o'clock. Everyone was indoors having high tea.

She parked at the manse and made her away over the fields at the back to the police station. It was dark and empty. She let herself in, praying that Hamish's pets were out somewhere. She was in luck. Nothing moved in the silence of the police station. She switched on a pencil torch and took out a fresh bottle of whisky. She took down a glass, put in a generous measure of whisky, and then poured laudanum into the glass and stirred it up.

Then she concealed herself at the side of the henhouse, waiting for Hamish to come home.

She heard the cat flap bang. She hoped one of the animals wouldn't come out again, sensing her presence. But Sonsie and Lugs were used to Josie by now and knew her smell and didn't bother to investigate.

The night was becoming frosty and she shivered, hoping Hamish would not be too long.

She heard the Land Rover drive up and Hamish's voice saying, "Come in, Elspeth. I couldnae believe my eyes when I saw you up at the hotel."

*   *   *

Elspeth followed Hamish into the kitchen. "I'll just go into the office and see if there are any messages," said Hamish.

"I am so tired," said Elspeth. "I drove all the way from Glasgow. I had to get away."

"Be with you in a minute," called Hamish. "There's a message here from one of my suspects."

Elspeth sat down wearily at the table. She picked up the glass of whisky and began to drink it. When she finished it, she rinsed out the glass and put it away.

"I'll light the stove," she shouted. But she suddenly felt very tired and disoriented. Before her dizzy eyes, she could see the lights of approaching cars that she had seen on her long drive up. She had got to her feet to light the stove, but she sat down again, put her head down on the table, and fell asleep.

Hamish came in and exclaimed, "Poor lassie. You're fair worn out."

Josie, crouched outside the kitchen window, saw him lift Elspeth in his arms and carry her through to the bedroom.

She had recognised Elspeth Grant. She had seen her many nights on television. But surely she was no competition. She was going to marry that actor.

Josie stumbled back across the fields. Before she entered the manse, she took a tube of extra-strong mints out of her pocket and began to chew two of them so that Mrs. Wellington would not smell whisky on her breath.

Elspeth awoke the next morning and stared around in a dazed way. She threw back the bedclothes. She was wearing only her underwear. What on earth was she doing in Hamish's bed?

Her skirt, blouse, and jacket were neatly arranged on a chair beside the bed. She took down Hamish's dressing gown from a hook at the back of the bedroom door and went in search of him.

Hamish was in the kitchen, notes spread out in front of him. "Morning, Elspeth," he said. "That must have been some drive. Sit down and I'll make coffee."

"I don't know what happened, Hamish," said Elspeth. "I helped myself to some of your whisky and then went out like a light."

"Never mind. You never told me what brought you up here." There was a tentative knock at the kitchen door. He opened it. Josie stood looking up at him and then past him to where Elspeth was sitting, wrapped in Hamish's dressing gown. She tried to enter but he blocked her way.

"Take the day off, McSween," he said. "I've got to go over my notes. I'll phone you if there's anything."

The door was firmly shut in Josie's face.

Josie craved a drink but did not want to buy too much whisky from Mr. Patel in case he gossiped. She got in her car and drove miserably off in the direction of Strathbane.

"So Elspeth," Hamish was saying. "Out with it."

She clutched the mug of coffee he had poured for her. "I had to get away from the press."

"But you *are* the press. You're a news presenter."

"I've broken off my engagement. I wanted it all to be quiet but Paul Darby's press agent got on to all the papers—I am sure with Paul's encouragement. He's very vain."

"So why did you get engaged to him?"

"I was on holiday in the Maldives. All that sun and being away from work and having a handsome man to squire me around. Do you remember when I got jilted at the altar by that fellow?"

"Yes."

"Well, from time to time, the papers drag that up. I suppose I wanted to show everyone that wee Elspeth Grant could do it. Paul's a big heartthrob. Of course, he works in England and I work in Scotland, so we had snatched time together, which added to the romance. Then his filming on the soap was over for a bit and he came up and moved in with me. Do you know, Hamish, his cosmetics took up more shelf space than mine?"

"What, make-up?"

"No, lotions and hair tonic and fake tan and God knows what else. There was little room for my clothes because he has such an extensive wardrobe. He expected me to play wifie and have meals ready for him and I just didn't have the time. I finally gave him back his ring. He tried to punch me so I tripped him up so that he fell on his bum. I told him if he ever laid a finger on me I'd call the police. He stormed off to see his press agent in London so I packed all his stuff up and left it with a neighbour, changed the locks, and left a note for him on the door. I had holiday time owing, so I just got in the car yesterday and drove straight to the Tommel Castle Hotel. I'd better beg Matthew not to put anything in the *Highland Times* or the press will follow me up here. They'll find out soon enough, but I want a few days' peace and quiet."

"I'll make us some breakfast but then I have to leave you,

Elspeth. It's this valentine murder. I have so many suspects, my head's going round and round. You look glamorous on the telly. Not now with your hair gone all frizzy again. But I like it frizzy."

"It can stay a mess while I'm here. I'm sick of hairdressers and beauticians. You know, Hamish, sometimes I wish I'd stuck to that job on the *Highland Times*. Never mind. Tell me about the case."

"I'll make breakfast first."

It was like old times, thought Hamish, as he put a plate of bacon and eggs in front of Elspeth. Elspeth looked like old times, too, with her frizzy hair and clear grey Gypsy eyes.

He began to go over the murder cases.

When he had finished, Elspeth said, "The main thing is background."

"Like what?"

"You need to dig and dig and find out if any of them have any knowledge in their past about how to make a letter bomb."

"Strathbane went through the lot. Nothing."

"But," said Elspeth, "have you got anyone on your list who came up after Strathbane checked?"

"There's a point. I've been checking on the men. I've only recently begun to check on the women."

"Now, someone young might not have had the experience," said Elspeth. "What about this Bill Freemont? Where's he gone?"

"I'll need to ask his wife. But he was checked."

"Maybe he knew someone who could do it for him."

"Good girl. I'll get over there and see the wife. Oh, I got a message from young Percy Stane. He thinks he's got something that might interest me. I'll call on him on the way back."

"Want me to come with you?"

Hamish hesitated and then said cautiously, "I suppose it'll be all right. Blair's given up and the press have gone. Mind, old rules! No reporting on anything unless I tell you to."

"Don't worry," said Elspeth. "I need a break."

The wildlife park had a lost, deserted air about it. Bad weather was moving in from the coast, carrying a metallic smell of snow to come on a rising wind.

Jocasta was not in the office and so they went up to the house, a small, squat, pebble-dashed bungalow.

Hamish rang the bell. Elspeth huddled behind him, the collar of her coat pulled up.

Jocasta answered the door. "What now?" she asked.

"Just a few questions."

"I don't want any newspeople around," said Jocasta, recognising Elspeth.

"Elspeth, wait in the car," said Hamish. When Elspeth had turned away, Hamish said, "Can I come in? It's freezing out here."

"Just for a minute," said Jocasta. "I'm packing things up." She ushered him into a cold living room full of packing cases.

"Do you know where your husband is?" asked Hamish.

"Unfortunately, I do. He had to give me an address to send on his stuff. I'll write it down for you. He's in Edinburgh."

Hamish waited until she had written down the address and handed it to him.

"Would you say that your husband was capable of making a letter bomb?"

"I would say that my husband was not capable of even mending a fuse," said Jocasta harshly.

"What about yourself?"

"The jealous wife? You can forget that. I was right off Bill even before I knew about Annie. In fact, I'm grateful to that conniving bitch. Makes it easy for me to get a divorce. What is a village bobby doing cruising around the countryside with a member of the rich and famous?"

"Do you mean Elspeth?"

"Who else?"

"Miss Grant is an old friend," said Hamish stiffly. "When you were packing up Bill's things, did you find anything like letters from Annie? Anything like that?"

"Nothing but a lot of unpaid bills that he said he had paid. Look, I am so fed up with him that if I had found there was even a hint of him being a murderer, I would have told you."

When Hamish hurried back to the Land Rover, snow was becoming to fall, small pellets driven before the wind.

"Any joy?" asked Elspeth.

"Nothing there," said Hamish. "We'd best get to Braikie while we can. The forecast is bad."

He drove north through the whitening landscape. "I forgot it could get like this," said Elspeth. "Yesterday was so glorious that I didn't remember that up here, you can get five climates in one day. It's getting worse. Are you sure you can see?"

"I'm all right. But I hope the gritters get their trucks out soon."

By the time they reached Braikie, the wind had dropped, but the snow continued to fall: large white Christmas card flakes, each one a miracle of cold lace.

At the town hall, they found that Percy was not in his office. Iona, at the switchboard, said he had stepped out half an hour ago.

They searched around Braikie in the pubs, in the café, and at the post office, but no one had seen Percy.

Their search was slowed by people recognising Elspeth and asking for autographs.

"Let's have something to eat," said Hamish, "and then find out where Percy lives."

They ate mutton pies and peas in the café and then drove back to the town hall. This time, Hamish asked Jessie Cormack if she knew where Percy had gone. She shook her head and said she had not seen him that morning. But she was able to give them his address.

Percy lived with his parents in a small, grey stone house on the outskirts of Braikie. A very thin woman with dyed blonde hair answered the door. She looked in alarm at Hamish. "Is my husband all right?"

"It's Percy I've come about," said Hamish. "He isn't in the office. Is he here?"

She shook her head. "Why are you asking about him?" she demanded. "Has he done something wrong?"

"Nothing like that. He left a message saying he had some information for me. Did he say anything to you?"

"He left this morning as usual." Her eyes widened in fear. "These murders! Do you think something has happened to my boy?"

"No, no. I am sure he will turn up. I'll phone you as soon as I find him."

"No joy," said Hamish when he joined Elspeth in the Land Rover. "Where the hell can he have gone? We'd best go back and sit in his office and see if he turns up. I'll need to let Sonsie and Lugs out for a run first."

"What's the point of having a great flap on your door if you're going to take your beasties everywhere with you?" demanded Elspeth.

"You never liked them," complained Hamish.

"I like them fine," said Elspeth. "But to have to look after two peculiar animals in a snowstorm when you're supposed to be detecting is ridiculous."

Hamish glared at her.

He let the dog and cat out of the back and stood huddled in his coat while they chased each other through the snow. At last he called them back and drove back to the town hall.

When they sat down in Percy's office, a bad-tempered silence reigned between them. Elspeth broke it by saying, "Now we're here, what about searching his desk?"

"Oh, all right," said Hamish sulkily.

He began to turn over every piece of paper on top of the desk and then began to go through the drawers. "There's something here," he said, holding up a videotape.

"Maybe Percy's back at the police station waiting for you," said Elspeth.

"I've got a video recorder. I'll just be leaving a receipt for this."

"I didn't think anyone had video recorders any more," said Elspeth.

"Well, now you know."

Chapter Nine

Whare sits our sulky, sullen dame,
Gathering her brows like gathering storm,
Nursing her wrath to keep it warm.

—Robert Burns

Back at the police station, Hamish, after he had lit the stove, said, "I'll make us a cup of coffee and then we'll have a look at this video. Strathbane won't get out the men to look for Percy because they say he's probably gone off somewhere with friends. I'll just need to hope he's all right and start searching in the morning."

The lights went out. "Damn," said Hamish. "The snow must have brought a cable down."

"I saw a face peering in at the window when the lights went out!" Elspeth exclaimed.

Hamish ran outside with the dog and cat at his heels. The snow had stopped, but it was freezing hard. He could hear it crunching under the feet of someone fleeing over the hill at the back. He set off in pursuit and brought the fleeing figure down in a rugby tackle.

"It's me, Josie," squeaked a frightened voice from under him.

Hamish pulled her to her feet. "What were you doing looking in at the kitchen window?" he demanded.

"I wanted to see what your instructions were for tomorrow," said Josie, close to tears. "I heard voices and thought I would look in the window and see if you were busy."

"You could have knocked," said Hamish angrily. "Get back to the manse and wait there until I phone you in the morning."

Hamish returned to the station. Elspeth had lit a hurricane lamp and placed it on the kitchen table.

"Who was it?" she asked.

"It was Josie McSween, my copper. She was running off up the back way. She said she heard voices and wanted to see who it was."

"Is she stalking you, Hamish? Where is she living?"

"Over at the manse."

"So what's she doing ploughing through the snow over the back way when she could have come round by the road?"

"She's a bit daft, that's all. It looks as if we aren't going to have a chance to see thon video."

"The hotel's got a generator."

"So it has. Let's go."

Hamish put out the lamp and lit a torch. "Hamish!" exclaimed Elspeth. "You don't have to let Sonsie and Lugs come with you. Leave them here for once. The kitchen's nice and warm.

"You can't go on with those beasts chained to you," she continued. "What woman would put up with rivals such as these?"

"You were aye jeering at them!"

"Don't let's quarrel," said Elspeth. "Let's get to the hotel."

They were about to drive off when the Currie sisters appeared, standing in the glare of the headlights and waving their arms. Hamish lowered the window. "What's up?"

"Tell Miss Grant the press are all at the hotel waiting for her," called Nessie.

"Waiting for her," chorused Jessie.

"Thanks," said Hamish.

He turned to Elspeth. "They'll all be in the bar. We'll park at the side and go in through the kitchen door."

The chef, Clarry, was sitting reading a newspaper when they entered the hotel kitchen.

"Evening, Hamish," he said. "I thought you pair might come in this way. Take the back stairs and the press won't see you. I'll send the boy up with some sandwiches. I've got some bones for Lugs and a bit o' fish for Sonsie. You can leave them here in the kitchen."

"She wouldnae let me bring them," said Hamish.

"Well, call in on your road out and I'll pack them up for ye."

Elspeth and Hamish made their way up the back stairs to Elspeth's room.

"Right," said Hamish. "Let's see what's on this video."

He switched on the television set and slid in the video.

It was a film of Annie being crowned Lammas queen. How faraway that sunny day appeared now! There he was, standing just below the platform. The provost raised the crown and placed it on Annie's head. She smiled triumphantly. Her two attendants were Jessie Cormack and Iona Sinclair. Jessie was glaring at Annie.

The film ran on. Percy had followed the procession through the town.

"Do you notice anything?" he asked Elspeth as he went to answer the door and receive a tray of food and coffee.

"It all looks ordinary," said Elspeth.

"Wait a bit," said Hamish. "Run it back a little. Stop! There! That's Jake from the disco. He's passing up a little package to her. Bastard! Dealing drugs right in the middle of what should ha' been an innocent day."

"Yes, but he's dead," said Elspeth. "I'm starving. Let's have something to eat and look through the tape again."

"I hope Percy's all right," Hamish fretted. He picked up the phone by the bed and called Percy's mother.

"He hasn't come home," she wailed. "Where's my boy?"

"We'll have a search party out in the morning," said Hamish. "I'll call as soon as I hear anything."

He then phoned Jimmy and explained the situation. "It's urgent, Jimmy," said Hamish. "Percy said he'd remembered something. Now he's missing."

"Can't do anything tonight, Hamish."

"I don't think I should wait until the morning, Jimmy.

Maybe I'll get over to Braikie and begin to look. I'll take McSween with me."

When he rang off, he said to Elspeth, "It's a right pity. I would ha' preferred your company, but the press'll be hounding you from now on."

"I know," said Elspeth sadly. "I'd better stop running away. I'll get back to Glasgow tomorrow where I've got a press agent to cope with the lot of them. I shouldn't have run away."

Hamish ejected the video. "When will you be back, Elspeth?"

"I don't know, Hamish. Maybe I'll spend my next holidays up here."

He bent his head to kiss her but the phone rang. Elspeth swore under her breath. She picked it up and then slammed it down again. Then she phoned reception and ordered that no calls were to be put through to her room.

Hamish hesitated in the doorway. "I'd better pack," said Elspeth, heaving her suitcase on the bed.

He felt he did not have the courage now to try to kiss her.

"You can't want a wee lassie like Josie to go out in this freezing cold," protested Mrs. Wellington when he arrived at the manse.

"It's her duty," said Hamish. "Go and get her."

Grumbling under her breath, Mrs. Wellington climbed the stairs to Josie's room and opened the door. The room was in darkness and there was a powerful reek of whisky. She switched on the light. Josie lay on the bed, fully dressed. She was snoring loudly. An empty whisky bottle lay on the floor beside the bed.

It's that Hamish Macbeth, thought Mrs. Wellington. He's driven the poor lassie to the bottle. I'll sort her out in the morning.

She went back downstairs. "Josie is very unwell," she said. "She has a bad cold and should rest."

"I'll see her tomorrow," said Hamish, thinking bitterly that Josie was absolutely useless.

Mrs. Wellington picked up the phone book and scanned the pages. Then she dialled a number. "Alcoholics Anonymous?" she asked. "When and where is your next meeting?"

The roads had been salted and gritted, and the Sutherland landscape lay dreaming whitely under a thick canopy of snow.

Hamish wondered where to start. He stopped in the main street in Braikie and checked his notebook for a list of phone numbers and addresses. He found the name Jessie Cormack. She lived with her parents in a flat above a greengrocer in a lane just off the main street.

He got out and walked there. He mounted the worn stone steps leading up from the street and rang the bell.

Jessie herself answered the door. "I was just about to go to bed," she said. "What's the matter? Is it Percy? Folks are saying he's disappeared."

"Can I come in?" Hamish removed his hat.

"You'd best come through to the kitchen," said Jessie. "My parents are watching television."

Hamish sat down and took out his notebook. "If Percy was worried about something, where would he go?"

She frowned in thought. "He might go to the minister."

"What about friends?"

"All his friends were from the kirk but he'd stopped seeing them and he barely spoke to me."

"Did Percy need money? If he thought he knew the killer, would he try to blackmail him?"

"Not Percy. He'd be more likely to do something stupid, like say to the murderer, 'I know it was you and I'm going to the police.'"

"That's what I'm afraid of."

Hamish drove to the minister's home. Martha Tallent opened the door. "What do you want?" she whispered. "Everyone's in bed."

"You'll do," said Hamish. "Just a wee word."

He followed her into the living room. "What's it about?" asked Martha.

"Have you seen anything of Percy Stane?"

"No. Why?"

"He phoned me to say he had some information and now he's missing."

Her eyes widened with shock. "Will this fright never end? He hasn't been here."

"Any phone calls?"

"Not for me. A few for Father. Nothing sinister. Just the usual parish business, people wanted to know about wedding and funeral arrangements and things like that."

"You heard them all?"

"Yes, we were all in the living room when they came in. I heard them all."

"Did you know Percy?"

"Only slightly. He was obsessed with Annie. Oh, I remember now. It was last week. Father went over to the Flemings' house to check the repairs to the kitchen and he found Percy loitering in the garden. When he asked what he was doing there, Percy said he wanted to be near the place she had died. Father told us he thought Percy was sick in the head and he wouldn't be at all surprised to learn that Percy was the murderer."

Hamish thanked her and went out again into the cold, frosty night. He went to the Flemings' home. The police tape had been removed. There was something pitiless about the biting cold and the white snow which blanketed everything. He cursed the "lambing blizzard" that often struck the Highlands in April.

The garden gate screeched when he opened it. He looked in the front windows of the house and then studied the front door. There was no sign of a break-in.

He made his way around the side of the house to the kitchen door. There was a new door and new windows; the kitchen door was locked and padlocked.

He turned and surveyed the garden, glittering under a small cold moon. His eyes narrowed as he saw a black lump of something in the far corner.

He switched on his torch and walked over, his boots crunching in the frozen snow.

Percy lay there, his dead eyes staring up at the uncaring moon. Blood from slashes in his wrists stained the snow. An old-fashioned cutthroat razor lay half buried in the snow beside him.

Hamish cursed under his breath. Poor Percy. What a waste of a young life. And all over some manipulative bitch! He had attended Annie's funeral but few people apart from the press had turned up. The locals, having learned of Annie's reputation, had shunned the funeral, which had taken place two whole months after her murder. None of the town's dignitaries who had smiled on her so fondly when she was the Lammas queen had bothered to put in an appearance. He retreated to his Land Rover, switched on the heater, took out his phone, and called Strathbane.

Then he waited. And as he waited, he began to wonder about Percy's death. Surely if Percy had planned suicide, he would not have bothered to phone the station in Lochdubh.

After a while, he heard the sound of approaching sirens. He was suddenly weary of the whole business. Percy's death had depressed him so much that his emotions felt as numb and as cold as the weather outside.

Jimmy Anderson was the first on the scene, followed by Andy MacNab. "Bad business," he said. "God, it's cold. Suicide?"

"Looks like it."

"Well, get your suit on and show me." They all struggled into their plastic suits. Hamish led the way to the garden. "We'll just stand here at the edge," said Jimmy. "Don't want to muck up the crime scene. I've called in a local doctor. Dr. Forsythe's retired and the nearest pathologist is in Aberdeen, would you believe it?"

Soon the garden was a hive of activity. A tent was erected over the body and halogen lights glared over the scene.

A local doctor, Dr. Friend, finished his examination. "Seems a clear case o' suicide," he said. "Poor young man."

"When you examined the cuts on his wrists," said Hamish, "did it look as if he'd really done it himself?"

"What are you getting at?" demanded Jimmy.

"Only that it seems odd to me," said Hamish. "The laddie phoned me earlier and said he had information for me. Now he's dead. Could someone have drugged him and then slashed his wrists for him?"

"I suppose it's possible. The pathologist will do a better estimation than me."

"There were no footprints near the body other than your own, Hamish," said Jimmy.

"So it happened earlier in the day. The falling snow would cover up any other footprints. Maybe we could have scraped off the top snow and seen if there was anything underneath but now everyone's trodden everything. Cutthroat razors aren't that common. I wonder if it could be traced."

"Hamish, you'll find it was suicide, plain and simple. You can go home now. There's nothing more we can do till we get a full postmortem. Do you want to tell his mother? Or shall I send a policewoman?"

"Send a policewoman," said Hamish gloomily.

"Where's McSween?"

"Ill in bed."

"I'll send Police Sergeant Sutherland. She's good at that sort of thing."

*   *   *

Hamish got home, feeling tired, cold, and miserable. Tomorrow the press who were waiting to see if they could interview Elspeth would be delighted to find they were all in the area of a murder. Press coverage meant pressure and pressure meant Blair.

Josie sat mutinously in Mrs. Wellington's car the following morning. She had been appalled to learn that the minister's wife was taking her to an AA meeting in Strathbane. Deaf to her protests, Mrs. Wellington had said that if Josie did not go, she would tell Hamish that Josie had been drunk. Mrs. Wellington had also found two precious half bottles of whisky in Josie's underwear drawer and confiscated them.

As the car neared Strathbane, Josie protested, "I'll be stuck in a room with smelly old drunks in dirty raincoats."

"It's where you belong," said the minister's wife. "But I happen to know respectable people go to these meetings."

She parked outside a church in the town centre. "There's a lunchtime meeting here. It's only an hour long. I'll see you inside and come back and pick you up when it's over."

A tall man in a business suit was standing at the door, acting as a greeter. "This is Josie," boomed Mrs. Wellington. "First meeting. Look after her."

"Will do. Come along, Josie. I'll introduce you. My name's Charlie."

There were twelve people in the room, all smartly dressed and clear-eyed. Josie would have felt better if they had been dirty old men. There was no one to feel superior to. They pressed literature on her and gave her a cup of tea. Then they all sat around a long table. A woman was the speaker. Josie mutinously did not listen to a word. What had it to do with her? What a stupid place and what stupid slogans pinned up on the walls—LIVE AND LET LIVE, EASY DOES IT, things like that. Stuff for morons, thought Josie.

But she pinned an interested look on her face, wondering all the time what Hamish was doing. Was he really interested in Elspeth? What chance had she compared with a television star? The newspapers said that Elspeth's engagement had broken off.

She realised with a start that the chairman was addressing her. "As it's your first meeting, Josie, you don't have to say anything."

"Thank you," she said. "I think you are all so brave."

It went round the room. People talked about free-floating anxiety, about loneliness of spirit, about selfishness. What has all this bollocks got to do with drink? thought Josie.

At last the dreadful meeting was over. People gave her phone numbers and wished her luck, along with a meeting list. Josie thanked them all and hurried out to where Mrs. Wellington was waiting for her.

"How did you get on, Josie?" she asked.

"Fine. Nice people. I've got a meeting list."

"Good girl. You'll be all right now."

Vodka, thought Josie. I'd best try vodka. It doesn't smell.

If she had been listening at the meeting she would have heard a woman say that she had started drinking vodka because she thought it would not smell and everyone had burst out laughing.

On the way back, her mobile rang. It was Hamish. "You're probably still in bed," he said. "I'm over in Braikie. Percy's dead."

"I need to get over to Braikie," said Josie. "There's been another death."

"This is horrible," said Mrs. Wellington. "Braikie is becoming like Chicago!"

When Josie arrived in Braikie, it was to find the small town full of policemen going door to door, but there was no sign of Hamish. She asked one if he had seen him and was told that Hamish was back in his police station.

Josie hurried back to Lochdubh. She went straight into the police station without knocking, a fact that Hamish, crouched over sheets of notes, noticed with annoyance.

"Next time, knock at the door," he snapped.

"I wondered what you wanted me to do today. I thought you would be in Braikie."

"I was," he said curtly. "But after chapping at a few doors as instructed by Blair and being told that the police had already been around, I thought I'd be better back here trying to figure out who killed Annie. Everything leads from the first murder."

"I'll help you," said Josie, starting to take off her coat.

"Good," said Hamish. "Get yourself over to Cnothan. There is a Mrs. Thomson, number nine, Waterway—that's down at the loch. She says she's been burgled but she has phoned before complaining about one thing or the other and it always turns out to be a figment of her imagination. Still, she sounded genuinely upset this time."

Josie trailed miserably off. Hamish had a sudden qualm of conscience. "Are you feeling better?" he called.

Josie came hurrying back. "I still feel a little weak."

"Help yourself to a coffee before you go. There's some on the stove."

"Can I bring you one?"

"What? Okay."

Josie happily busied herself in the kitchen, looking about herself with possessive eyes. The kitchen was too small. It could be extended. Copper pans, hanging on hooks, she thought dreamily.

She took Hamish a mug of coffee. He leaned back in his chair and wrinkled his nose. "Have you been drinking vodka?"

"No!" exclaimed Josie, feigning outrage.

Hamish shrugged. "Smells like it to me. Drink your coffee and get over to Cnothan."

Josie put her own mug down on the desk next to his and pulled up a chair.

"Take your coffee into the kitchen," ordered Hamish.

Josie trailed off. He just didn't know what was good for him, she thought. The cat suddenly looked up at her with yellow eyes and gave a low hiss. I'd better make friends with those animals, thought Josie. I'll start to bring them food. If I drug Hamish, I'll need to drug them as well.

*   *   *

The days for Hamish crawled past as he waited for the autopsy report. Finally Jimmy called. "This is a right mess," he said. "There was a quantity of sleeping drug in the boy's stomach along with a lot of whisky. The pathologist says that from the angles of the cuts, it looks as if someone did it for him. Have you worked out anything at all, Hamish? We're getting desperate."

"I found a video in his desk."

"Have you been withholding evidence?"

"There was nothing on it but mair evidence of Percy's obsession with Annie. It was a video of her as the Lammas queen last summer."

"I'm coming over to see it," said Jimmy.

"Meet me at the hotel then," said Hamish. "I have a video machine here but I tried it last night and it wasnae working."

Mr. Johnson let them use one of the hotel rooms. Once more the sunny scene sprang into view. "Thon provost seems pretty friendly," said Jimmy. "See the way he presses his big fat hand on her shoulder?"

The tape ran to the end. Hamish switched it off. They sat looking at each other gloomily while the melting snow outside dripped from the eaves like tears.

"Wasted journey," complained Jimmy. "I'll take this tape with me. I'll slide it into the evidence locker. You know Blair. Even if this is of no importance, he would use your withholding evidence to suspend you. Where's McSween?"

"Over at Cnothan on a burglary."

"She's a bonnie lass, Hamish. You could do worse."

"She haunts me. I always get the feeling that she's *brooding* over me."

"Och, man, that's just male vanity."

"Maybe. She's probably making a pig's breakfast of the investigation."

But Josie was determined to do things properly. To her surprise, she found there was definite evidence of a break-in. The back door had been jimmied open. She phoned Strathbane for a forensic team but the name of Mrs. Thomson was well known and Josie was told they had nobody to spare. So she got a fingerprint kit out of her car and dusted for prints. Mrs. Thomson had kept the missing money in a drawer by her bed. Josie lifted two good fingerprints from the drawer and rushed the evidence to Strathbane, where she trawled the fingerprint files on the computer. Her eyes lit up when she got a match.

Jimmy had just arrived back when Josie triumphantly showed him the evidence. The culprit was Derry Harris, a local Cnothan layabout. Jimmy passed the news to Police Inspector Ettrick, who got two police officers to go back to Cnothan with Josie and make the arrest. The money was recovered, and Josie basked in the inspector's praise.

She arrived at the police station in Lochdubh that evening with a packet of fish for Sonsie and a packet of lamb's liver for Lugs.

Hamish listened while she described the solving of the burglary. "Good girl!" he said. "Well done!" Josie glowed.

"I suppose you'll be going to the wedding on Saturday."

"What wedding?" asked Josie.

"Muriel McJamieson is marrying John Bean. They are both villagers so everyone's invited. I'm surprised Mrs. Wellington hasn't told you."

The truth was that Josie had seen as little of Mrs. Wellington as possible, telling that lady every evening that she was off to a meeting. Her brain raced. There would be drinking at the wedding. She would need to make sure Hamish had a few drinks and then lure him back to the station and drug him.

She realised for the first time that if she appeared cold and detached, Hamish would drop his guard.

So she said casually, "I'll think about it. I'll be on my way, sir."

She's turning out all right after all, thought Hamish.

Josie drove up to the Tommel Castle Hotel and asked if Elspeth was still there.

"She's hiding in her room," said Mr. Johnson. "She's leaving in the morning."

"May I have a word with her?" asked Josie.

The manager looked at her doubtfully. "Is it police business?"

"No, just a wee chat."

"I'll phone her."

He rang Elspeth's room and said, "Policewoman McSween is downstairs and wants a word with you. No, it's not police business."

He put down the phone and said, "You can go up. Room twenty-one."

Elspeth answered the door and looked curiously at Josie. "What is it?" she asked. "Is Hamish all right?"

"I just wanted to ask your advice."

"Come in."

Josie sat down on the bed and looked up earnestly with her big brown eyes at Elspeth.

"You are a woman of the world," began Josie.

A line from a Gilbert and Sullivan operetta flashed into Elspeth's brain: "Uttering platitudes / In stained glass attitudes."

"What's that got to do with anything?" she asked.

"I'm old-fashioned," said Josie piously. "Not like you. If a man sleeps with me, do you think he ought to marry me?"

"Are we talking about Hamish?" asked Elspeth.

"I didn't say that."

"Well, these days, women must take responsibility as well as men. Unless you've been raped, you haven't a hope in hell if it was only a one-night stand." Elspeth's face hardened. "Now, if you'll excuse me, I have packing to do. I suggest you consult a professional."

She went and held open the door.

Josie left, burning up with fury. What did she know about anything? But Josie hoped that Elspeth would think that she had meant Hamish.

Hamish lay in bed that night, reading a detective story. He sighed as he finally put the book down. Fictional detectives never seemed to be hit with long days and weeks of not having a clue. "I'd give anything for even a red herring," he said to his pets before he switched out the light. His last gloomy thought before he went to sleep was that Blair would hound and hound until he found any suspect.

Josie craved a drink. She had been frightened to hide any more in her room in case Mrs. Wellington found the bottles. Without a drink, she felt she could not go through with the plan of trapping Hamish.

She had a bottle of vodka hidden under the roots of a rowan tree in the garden. Josie waited and waited until she was sure her hosts would be safely asleep. She crept along the corridors. So many rooms and the Wellingtons childless! The manse had been built in the days of enormous families. Down the stairs, treading carefully over the second one from the bottom that creaked, out into the blustery cold, taking out a pencil torch and heading rapidly for the rowan went Josie. She scrabbled in the roots of the tree until her fingers closed over the vodka bottle.

Holding it to her chest, she scurried back to the manse. As she got to the foot of the stairs, she noticed that the light was on in the landing. Glad she was still in uniform, she stuffed the bottle into an inside pocket of her coat. Mrs. Wellington was coming out of the bathroom. "I forgot to take my sleeping pill," she said. "Goodness, you're late."

"I went for coffee with some people after the meeting," said Josie.

"Oh, good girl! Night, night."

"Good night," said Josie, scuttling down the corridor to her room.

She was just about to unscrew the top of the bottle when she heard footsteps approaching along the corridor outside. Josie thrust the bottle under the mattress, whipped off her coat, and began to pull her regulation sweater over her head as the door opened.

"Oh, sorry," said Mrs. Wellington. "I just came to ask you if you'd like a hot-water bag."

"No thanks," said Josie. "I'm fine."

"Right. See you in the morning."

Josie waited again until she heard the door of Mrs. Wellington's room shut. Her hands were shaking. She seized the bottle from under the mattress and twisted off the top. She drank a great mouthful, feeling the spirit burn down to her stomach and a glow beginning to spread through her body.

Josie sat down by the fire that Mrs. Wellington had lit earlier and began to drink steadily.

Chapter Ten

☠

Life is just one damned thing after another.

—Elbert Hubbard

Josie awoke the next day and felt she had not thought the drugging of Hamish through properly. If she used laudanum or Mandrax then he might remember clearly what happened before he went to sleep. Rohypnol, that date-rape drug, was the answer. But how could she get hold of some? There had been a case of a girl claiming she had been drugged and raped. What had been her name? Grace something or other. Think!

She phoned Hamish and said she had some shopping to do in Strathbane. "Go ahead," said Hamish. "There's nothing more we can do at the moment. But keep away from police headquarters!"

Josie drove to the library at Strathbane and by trawling through the back numbers of the *Strathbane Journal* on the library computer, she found the name she was looking for—Grace Chalmers.

Now the problem was how to get the Chalmers evidence box without signing for it. Somehow, she would have to try to con her way into where the evidence was kept.

She knew old Joe Macdonald, in charge of the evidence room, had a soft spot for her.

But when she made her way downstairs, she saw to her dismay that the man on the other side of the counter was Charlie, the greeter from the AA meeting.

"Why, Josie," he said. "I didnae know we were both in the same business. How are you getting on?"

"Where's Joe?"

"Oh, he's retired."

Josie thought quickly. "Can I come through and talk to you?"

"I shouldnae, really, but och, I'm supposed to help a fellow sufferer. Come on through."

He buzzed her in. "Having trouble wi' John Barleycorn?" he asked.

"Just a bit."

"Which meetings do you . . . Damn, there's someone coming. Hide yourself."

Josie darted behind the shelves of evidence boxes and began to search desperately. At last she found the box she was looking for and opened it up. There was a bottle of Rohypnol in its evidence bag, all neatly labelled. She stuffed it quickly in her pocket. She heard Charlie calling her and went back to the desk.

"Josie," he said urgently, "get back outside. You have my number. Give me a ring."

"Will do," said Josie.

Once she was back outside, he asked, "Now what was it you wanted?"

"I wanted to look at evidence from the Percy Stane murder."

"Then you'll need to go over to forensics. It's all still there."

Josie thanked him and made her escape.

Her head was full of plans as she drove back to Lochdubh. No more booze. She was not an alcoholic. She would need a clear head. She must get into the police station just before the wedding reception and drug those wretched animals. Some laudanum in their drinking bowls should do the trick. Then she'd better put the Rohypnol in Hamish's drink at the wedding reception. Maybe make sure it was a soft drink. It could be lethal in alcohol.

Saturday dawned bright and sunny. The wedding service was to be held at eleven o'clock in the morning. Then there was a wedding breakfast for close friends and family and at seven in the evening in the village hall, there was to be a grand party for everyone in the village and round about who cared to come.

The wedding service went well but Hamish wasn't there. Outside the church, Josie phoned Hamish's mobile. He said he was over in Braikie but would be back for the dance and told her to enjoy herself.

Carrying a packet of fish and a packet of venison, Josie let herself into the police station at six o'clock. She fed the dog and the cat and then poured laudanum into their drinking bowls and made her way back to the manse to change for the party.

She decided to wear a conservative black dress with a choker of pearls. She meant to look as respectable as possible.

It was just when she was about to leave her room that the whole plan appeared to her to be dangerous and stupid. What had come over her? Her hands began to shake. She rolled back the rug and prised up a loose floorboard where she had hidden a bottle of Scotch. She gulped some down and then some more.

No, she thought stubbornly, Hamish and I are meant to be together. Like a soldier going off to battle, she hid the bottle, stood up, squared her shoulders, and marched to the door.

When she arrived at the church, the bride, resplendent in her wedding dress, was taking the floor with her new husband. Josie's eyes filled with sentimental tears. That will soon be me, she thought.

She helped herself to a soft drink, aware of Mrs. Wellington's eyes on her. Josie accepted several offers to dance, all the time watching the door for the arrival of Hamish.

At last she saw his fiery head. He was impeccably dressed in his one good suit. Josie went to join him. "How is it going?" she asked.

"Still nothing," said Hamish. "Let's find a quiet corner. I want to talk about it."

They both walked to a corner of the hall, away from the band. "It's thon damn video," complained Hamish. "I've watched it and watched it until my eyes hurt. There must be something there. I've even borrowed a machine from the hotel so I can go over it at the police station."

"Perhaps I could have a look at it this evening," said Josie. "Maybe a fresh pair of eyes is what you need."

"You won't want to miss the fun."

"I don't mind."

"All right. We'll have something to eat. I've got to talk to a few people and thank Grace's parents for the party. I'll let you know when I'm ready to go."

This was all meant to happen, thought Josie.

She sat in a corner of the hall, refusing offers to dance, frightened that Hamish might think she was enjoying herself so much that he would leave her behind.

But he finally came up to her and said, "Are you sure you can be bothered looking at that video tonight?"

"Yes, I'm dying to see it," said Josie eagerly.

Curious eyes watched them leave the hall together.

At the police station, Hamish exclaimed, "Would you look at those lazy beasts!" Sonsie and Lugs lay curled up together asleep beside the stove. "Now come into the living room, and I'll run that video."

"Can I get you something to drink?" asked Josie.

"Not at the moment."

She followed him into the living room. She shivered. Hamish had central heating but hardly ever used it.

Hamish switched on the television and slotted the video in. Josie decided to pay close attention. If she did find something, he would be so thrilled with her that it would throw him off-guard.

What if there might be someone amongst the crowd that

Hamish had not noticed? So instead of studying the main characters, she kept her eyes on the audience. The Lammas queen was crowned and proceeded on a float through the town, then back to the field.

Suddenly she leaned forward. "Stop the film! Right, run it back a bit. Stop! There! At the edge of the screen."

The provost and councillors had left the rostrum, where the queen now sat with her attendants. It was a back view. Percy had moved behind the rostrum to film the crowds.

The provost and councillors stood in groups near the rostrum, chatting. At the very edge of the screen stood Jamie Baxter. He was looking straight at Annie, and his face was a mask of hatred. Hamish ran the film slowly forward. His wife was with him. She said something to him and tugged at his arm, and then they both walked away.

"Well, I neffer," breathed Hamish, the sibilance of his accent showing his excitement. "I wonder if there's anything in our Jamie's background to show he knew about bombs. I'll check tomorrow. Oh, good girl! This calls for a drink."

"I'll get it," said Josie. "Whisky."

"Aye, but put a lot of water in it. I want to have a clear head in the morning. The bottle's in the cupboard. I'll chust hae a look at this again."

Josie hesitated in the kitchen. He was pleased with her. Let it go. But what if Elspeth came back from Glasgow? According to Mrs. Wellington, they'd been an item.

She took down the bottle of whisky and poured a weak measure for Hamish and a strong one for herself. She added two crushed tablets of Rohypnol to Hamish's drink and stirred them up.

"Switch off the light," ordered Hamish. "I want a better look at this."

Everything's going my way, thought Josie. If there're any grounds in the glass, he won't notice in the dark. She handed Hamish his drink. "Slainte," she said.

Hamish took a drink. "You're right," he said, his eyes glued to the screen. "How could I ha' missed that?"

He continued drinking while he stared at the screen. Then he suddenly put his hand up to his head. "I feel dizzy."

"Maybe there was something in the food at the party," said Josie. Hamish stood up and swayed.

"Let me get you to bed." She supported his lanky figure as he stumbled towards the bedroom.

Hamish fell on the bed. When he had come back to the police station, he had taken off his jacket and tie. Josie struggled until she had removed his shirt. His eyes were closed, and he seemed to be out cold. She threw the shirt on the floor and then pulled his trousers off. By the time she got his underpants and socks and shoes off, she was sweating. There was the final effort of managing to get him under the bedclothes. She stripped off her own clothes and crept naked into the bed beside him. She rubbed her naked body against his, working herself up. There must be a smell of sex when he woke up in the morning.

This is what it's going to be like for real, thought Josie, laying her head on his chest.

*   *   *

Hamish slowly regained consciousness the following morning. He felt a body next to his. He blearily looked down into Josie's sleeping face. He rolled out of bed and fell on the floor with a thump. He stared down at his naked body. A trail of discarded clothes lay on the floor from the entrance to the bedroom to the bed.

He clutched his forehead and groaned aloud. Josie became awake. "Good morning, darling," she said huskily.

Hamish seized the duvet from the bed and covered his naked body. That left Josie exposed. He stumbled to his feet, grabbed his dressing gown, and wrapped it around himself. He went into the kitchen where his bleary animals were just waking up. He lit the stove with trembling hands and put water on to boil for coffee.

Josie came up behind him and put her arms around him. "Get off!" snarled Hamish.

"But, Hamish, darling," wailed Josie. "After last night, you can't treat me like this."

"I cannae remember a thing," muttered Hamish. "Look, if this gets out, we'll lose our jobs. Keep your mouth shut and forget it effer happened."

"But I can't. I love you."

"Josie, just go. If it was a one-night stand, I'm sorry. It won't happen again. Take yourself off to your mother's and leave me in peace for a bit. Maybe some bastard gave me a mickey at that party. I'll go to Brodie and get a blood test taken and then go over to forensics and get them to analyse it."

Tears running down her face, Josie dressed, put on her coat, and staggered from the police station. This was a nightmare.

It would all lead back to her, she was sure of it. Hamish would soon realise she was the one who was interested in drugging him.

To her relief, Mrs. Wellington was out when she got back to the manse. Josie packed her suitcase, went downstairs, and left a note on the kitchen table for Mrs. Wellington before going out to her car and driving off, squinting through her tears.

Hamish hurried to Dr. Brodie's surgery and got the doctor to take a blood test and a urine sample. "Give them to me," ordered Hamish, "and I'll take them over to forensics."

"Hamish, no one else at the wedding has been in here to complain of any ill effects."

Hamish drove quickly to the forensics lab. Lesley regarded him impatiently when she heard his request. "We're backed up, Hamish. You should have left the doctor to send them to the hospital lab."

"Chust dae this," snapped Hamish. "Someone tried to drug me. I'm sure of it."

"Oh, leave it," said Lesley. "We'll do our best."

When Hamish had left, her husband, Bruce, asked, "What was that about?"

"Hamish has left us his blood sample and urine sample. He wants a rush on it. He thinks he's been drugged."

"We've got too much to do," said Bruce, who was jealous of Hamish because he knew his wife had at one time been keen on the policeman. "Shove them in the fridge."

"But what do I tell him when he starts nagging on the phone?"

"Oh, for heaven's sakes, tell him he's clear. We can't be wasting time on one damn highland policeman."

Hamish stood outside the lab and phoned Jimmy. "Where are you?" he asked.

"I'm in the pub."

"It isn't even noon yet!"

"What are you? The Temperance Society?"

"I'm coming to see you. I've got a breakthrough."

"It's the pub next to headquarters."

"What if Blair finds me there?"

"He won't. He's down at the docks."

Jimmy was sitting at a corner table in the pub. "What's all the excitement about?"

Hamish told him about the tape and about the look on Jamie Baxter's face.

"Och, come on, laddie!" said Jimmy when he had finished. "He's a respectable man wi' an impeccable background."

"What is his background?" asked Hamish. "You told me you had checked all my suspects."

"He was in special forces in Northern Ireland."

"Was he now? Jimmy, what better place to find out all about bomb making? Didn't you connect the dots? You should ha' told me about this. I want a warrant."

"You'll need a lot more evidence to get a warrant than a look on a man's face months ago."

"I'm going over to have a word wi' him."

"Well, mind how you go and if the shit hits the fan and he

starts howling to Daviot, I'll swear blind it's the first I've heard of it."

At the town hall, Hamish asked Jessie Cormack where her boss was. "He's gone to Edinburgh with his wife," said Jessie. "There's some function or other they have to attend."

Hamish went back outside and climbed into his Land Rover. He had to get inside Jamie's house.

Dressed in black, he left his police station that night at two in the morning. He had borrowed an old Volvo from Iain at the garage, not wanting the Land Rover to be seen anywhere near the Baxters' house.

It was a dark, cold, misty night. He parked the Volvo some distance away and made his way along a lane at the back of the Baxters' house. The garden gate was locked but he climbed nimbly over it and dropped down into the garden. He had not noticed any sign of a burglar alarm on his previous visits to Cora. He opened a small backpack, took out his forensic coveralls, and put them on, even covering his boots. He did not want any trace of him to be found in the house.

He took out a ring of skeleton keys and got to work on the back door, hoping it was not bolted on the other side. Householders often did not realise how effective a bolt could be.

At last the lock clicked open and he slid quietly into the kitchen. His pencil torch flickered over the sterile kitchen's gleaming surfaces. He made his way from the kitchen into a square hall. He looked briefly into the downstairs living room and dining room before making his way quietly up the stairs. He hoped Jamie had a study.

He found it beside the main bedroom. Thanking his stars the study was at the back of the house, he sat down at Jamie's desk and began to go through the drawers. The bottom one was locked. He worked steadily with a skeleton key, not wanting to force the drawer. His heart sank when all he found were pornographic magazines and a bottle of whisky.

He flicked the torchlight around the room. There was a small wall safe. If there is anything incriminating, it will be in there, thought Hamish. But how to get the combination?

He searched the desk again, hoping that Jamie might have written the combination somewhere. He took out all the drawers and looked at the back. Nothing. He replaced the drawers and switched on Jamie's computer. There was a file for addresses and telephone numbers. He opened it up. He recognised Annie's home number and work number. He studied all the names and was about to give up when he saw a name in the middle—McPeter. *Peter* was slang for "safe." Beside it were six numbers with the area code for Braikie. He knew a lot of people tried to keep numbers secure by making them look like a phone number. He scribbled the number in a small notebook and then went over to the safe.

He moved the dial, squinting down at the numbers he had written. He let out a low whistle of satisfaction when the door swung open. Inside were various letters from building contractors. It seemed as if Jamie had been giving contracts to friends for a payoff. There was a manila envelope. He pulled it out and took it over to the desk. Inside was a smaller envelope containing photographs. He slid them out. They were of Annie, either naked or wearing fishnet stockings and a suspender belt. He put them to one side and studied the rest of the contents. There was a book on bomb making.

He went back to the safe and pulled out a metal box. He took it to the desk and opened it. Inside was a cutthroat razor and bottles of chemicals. The fool, thought Hamish. The vain murderous fool! He was *proud* of what he had done. He probably sat in his office, gloating over his trophies.

Hamish spread all his finds on the desk, risked switching on the lights, and, taking out a small, powerful digital camera, began to photograph the evidence. Then he carefully put everything back the way it was and locked the safe.

Mr. Patel was roused at seven in the morning by Hamish hammering on the door of his flat above the shop. "What is it, Hamish?" he asked.

"I need to use that machine in the shop for printing photos."

"At this time o' the day?"

"It iss top secret."

"Oh, come round to the front and I'll let you in."

In the shop, Hamish slid the memory card into the machine and then waited while the photos were printed off. He had told Mr. Patel not to look.

"I hope that all did ye some good," said Mr. Patel when he had finished. "I just hope it isnae your holiday photos."

"I've forgotten what a holiday's like," said Hamish. "I'll take a packet o' these manila envelopes."

*   *   *

Hamish went back to the police station and, still wearing latex gloves, wrote SUPERINTENDENT DAVIOT in block capitals on an envelope, addressed it, and then put all the photographic evidence inside. He typed out a note: "Evidence from Jamie Baxter's safe." He steamed off an old stamp and put it on the envelope.

He couldn't bear to post it and have to wait until it was delivered, fearing that Jamie would destroy everything before a search warrant could be issued. He went through to his bedroom, wrinkling his nose in distaste at the faint smell of sex from his bed, and rummaged under the bed where he kept a box with some disguises. He selected a black wig, glasses, a black moustache, and a cap. He changed out of his regulation boots and put on an old pair of trainers.

Lugs and Sonsie looked at him hopefully but he said, "Be good. I won't be long." The animals eyed him curiously as he put on his disguise.

He opened the kitchen door and peered out. Nobody was around. He got into the Volvo and drove off to Strathbane. He parked some way away from police headquarters and then walked towards the building.

To his delight, he saw a postman just getting out of his van. As the postman walked towards the building, carrying a pile of mail fastened with a rubber band, Hamish called to him. "You've dropped one."

He handed the postman the envelope. "I don't know how that could have happened," said the postman. "But thanks."

Hamish went back to Lochdubh, stopping on the way to

strip off his disguise and the clothes. He left the car at the garage in the village. Back at the police station, he got an old oil drum out of the shed and put the disguise in it. He went in, changed into his uniform, got his forensic suit and boots, and threw them in as well. He added the clothes he had been wearing when he had broken into the Baxters' home. On a sudden impulse he ran indoors and stripped his bed and stuffed the sheets and pillowslips on top. Then he remembered the memory card from his camera. He added that as well. He poured petrol over the lot and set it on fire.

He was suddenly exhausted, and that exhaustion brought back unhappy memories of waking up next to Josie. When everything in the oil drum had burnt down to black ash, he went indoors. He put his head down on the kitchen table and fell asleep.

He was awakened three hours later by the shrilling of the phone. He struggled to his feet and went to answer it. It was Jimmy. "Hamish, we've got evidence on Jamie Baxter. We're heading over there with a warrant. Want to be in at the kill?"

"I'll be there as quick as I can."

"You weren't breaking and entering last night by any chance?"

"Would I ever? See you soon."

Cora was driving as the black BMW moved into the Baxters' street. "Wake up, Jamie," she said, nudging her husband in the passenger seat. "What are all these policemen doing outside our house? Oh, stop them! They're about to break the door down!"

But Daviot had seen their car arriving and told the men with the battering ram to wait.

Jamie got slowly out of the car followed by his wife. "What is going on here?" he demanded.

Daviot handed him a search warrant. "Open up," he said. "You wait here, Mrs. Baxter. A policewoman will look after you."

Hamish drove up just as Jamie was being ushered into his home. Cora looked at him, her eyes blazing with hatred. "You!" she spat out.

He walked into the house and straight up the stairs to the office. Daviot was standing in front of the safe, flanked by Blair. "Open it!" he ordered Jamie.

Jamie gave a grin like a rictus and patted his pockets. "I lost the combination. I meant to get on to the company, and—"

"Stop havering, man," yelled Blair. "Open the damn thing or we can all wait here till I get someone to blast it open."

Jamie's shoulders sagged. He twisted the dial, and the safe swung open. He stood, head hanging, as Daviot went through the contents. He held up the cutthroat razor.

"If I might have a look," said Hamish.

"Get back to your sheep and leave this tae the experts," said Blair.

"What is it, Macbeth?" asked Daviot as Hamish drew on a pair of latex gloves and took out a powerful magnifying glass. He studied the razor. "There's a bit o' blood just between the handle and the blade," said Hamish. "If you get that examined, you'll probably find it's Percy Stane's."

Daviot charged Jamie with three murders. He was led outside. He saw his wife and screamed, "You bitch! You told them!"

Daviot said wearily to Blair, "Charge Mrs. Baxter with being an accomplice. Take her in for questioning."

Jimmy drew Hamish aside. "Was it you that sent the photos?"

"What photos?" asked Hamish. "Listen, put in a word for wee Josie. If it hadnae been for her sharp eyes, I'd never have got on to Jamie."

"Are you coming back to Strathbane for the interviews?"

"No, I'm going back home. Thank God, it's all over," said Hamish Macbeth, blissfully unaware that trouble of another sort was looming on his horizon.

When he got back to the police station, he phoned the forensic lab and spoke to Bruce. "Have you got my results?"

Bruce had just been phoned to stand by for a rush job on the razor. Why should he bother with a pillock like Hamish? So he said, "We checked them. Nothing at all."

"Nothing!"

"Clean as a whistle."

Hamish rang off and stared miserably into space. He realised that he had recently come to the conclusion that Josie had drugged him. How else would he have gone to bed with her?

Flora was worried about her daughter. Josie kept mostly to her room, playing dreary pop tunes over and over again. She did not know that Josie was waiting in dread for the results of Hamish's tests.

So that when her mother climbed the stairs to tell her Hamish was on the phone, she turned chalk white. But she decided she had better get it over with.

She went slowly down the stairs and picked up the phone. "Hullo," she said in a shaky voice.

"Good news," said Hamish. "We've cleared up the murders and it's all thanks to you. We got Baxter this morning. When are you coming back?"

"Have you had the result of those tests?"

"Yes, I got them and there's nothing there. Look, I'm awfy sorry. I don't know what came over me. Let's chust forget the whole thing."

"I'll be back tomorrow," said Josie.

Her mother was amazed at the transformation in her daughter. Josie's eyes were shining, and colour had returned to her face.

"What did he say?" she asked.

"He said it's thanks to me those dreadful murders have been solved."

"Oh, so that's what's been hanging over my wee girl. Maybe you're just not suited to the force, Josie. All those dreadful deaths! Why don't you get out the house? Go and see Charlotte. You used to be such friends."

"I'll do that," said Josie, thinking of Charlotte's generous drinks cabinet. Flora had begun to suspect her daughter was drinking too much and so there was no liquor in the house.

Josie made her way to her friend's home. Charlotte had recently got married to a local builder. To Josie, Charlotte's bungalow seemed like a dream, from its ruched curtains at the windows to the fitted carpets throughout.

Charlotte, a chubby, cheerful girl, hugged Josie and said, "You're just in time."

"What for?"

"I'm about to crack open a bottle of champagne. I'm pregnant. I got one of those kits that advertises it can tell you you're pregnant before you know it yourself. See! Look at that blue line. You sit down, pet, and I'll open the champers." Charlotte opened the door of the drinks cabinet and the tinkling strains of "Highland Laddie" filled the room. Josie stared down at the pregnancy kit as if mesmerised. If only Hamish had really seduced her and she had got pregnant, he'd need to do the honourable thing.

"Here you are," said Charlotte, handing her a glass.

"Congratulations," said Josie. She took a gulp of champagne and felt the relief of having alcohol once more coursing through her body.

She had been to school with Charlotte and so they drank and talked about former school friends.

A car drew up outside. "That's my Bill!" said Charlotte and ran out to meet him.

Josie opened her handbag and slid the pregnancy kit inside.

When they came in, arm and arm, Josie got to her feet. "I'll leave you to it," she said. "Congratulations again."

"Let me show you the pregnancy kit," said Charlotte. "Damn. Where is it? I'm so excited I can't remember where I put it.

Never mind. I've made an appointment with the doctor tomorrow to get it confirmed."

"Should you be drinking?" asked Bill.

"I'm going to get right blootered and then I'm not going to drink another thing until the baby is born. Open up another bottle!"

Josie stopped at the supermarket where they sold bags of ice. In her car outside, she dropped the kit into the ice, wrapped in a polythene bag. The day was freezing so she hid the bag in the garage.

Hamish phoned Jimmy the next day. Josie had arrived and he had told her to do the rounds of the faraway areas. "So did he confess?" asked Hamish.

"That he did. When we told him his wife had turned on him, he cracked. I think he's a haggis supper short o' the neeps. He was obsessed wi' Annie and added to that he's as arrogant as the devil. She lost interest in him and he decided to get rid of her in the nastiest way he could think of."

"What about Cora? Has she been charged as an accomplice?"

"She has. But she'll get off lightly. She'll even make bail."

"Why?"

"She said she was terrified of him."

"Nothing terrifies a woman like Cora."

"Hamish, the poor woman was married to a triple murderer. She said she couldn't bear it any longer so it was she who sent in yon package of photos."

"I don't believe it for a minute."

"Well, that's what she's saying. Wasn't you, was it?"

Hamish thought quickly. It would do no good to tell Jimmy the truth because in order to prove Cora wrong, he would need to admit to having broken into the Baxters' home.

"Me? Not on your life," he said.

But privately he thought that Cora had been in the grip of an obsession almost as mad as that of her husband. Respectability and her position as a councillor's wife was her life and the very air she breathed.

Hamish found Josie good company in the weeks that followed. Josie cunningly knew instinctively that if she betrayed any romantic feelings towards Hamish, then he would back off. He even took her out for dinner a couple of times. The villagers thought they were watching a budding romance, and hadn't Mrs. Wellington said she was sure there would soon be a wedding?

Meanwhile, Josie laid her plans. She had paid over one thousand pounds to a shady doctor in Strathbane to give her a certificate saying she was pregnant.

Just as the snows were beginning to melt and a balmy wind was bringing the first hint of spring, she called at the police station.

"Hamish, I'm pregnant," she said.

Chapter Eleven

Their tricks and craft hae put me daft,
They've ta'en me in, an' a' that

—Robert Burns

The news of Hamish's Macbeth's engagement to Josie Mc-
Sween was greeted with delight in the village of Lochdubh.
They were such a *suitable* couple. She was a pretty wee lassie and
a policewoman, too.

Only Angela Brodie was worried. One evening, shortly after
the announcement of Hamish's engagement, her husband con-
fided in her that Hamish had come to him one morning, demanding a drug test, but that the forensic lab had stated that
he was clear.

She knew Hamish better than most. Although he smiled
on Josie and escorted her about, Angela sensed a bleakness in
him. She didn't like Josie. She thought there was something sly
about her.

Also, Hamish, who usually dropped in for a chat, had been

avoiding her. She found him one morning, leaning on the wall overlooking the loch, with his animals at his heels.

"Hamish!" she hailed him. "I haven't had a chance to talk to you. So you're finally going to be married? Congratulations."

"That iss verra kind of you, Angela." His eyes were flat and guarded. "I'd had best be getting along to the station."

"Wait a moment. Are you happy?"

"Of course," said Hamish, and he strode off.

Angela was walking back home when she met Mrs. Wellington. "Isn't it exciting?" said the minister's wife. "I've come to think of Josie as my own daughter."

"I don't think Hamish is very happy," said Angela.

"It doesn't matter if he's happy or not. He got the girl preg . . ." Mrs. Wellington actually blushed.

"Do you mean Josie's pregnant?"

"Don't tell a soul. I shouldn't have said anything."

"I don't think Josie is my husband's patient."

"Well, no. It would spoil the occasion if people thought it was a shotgun wedding."

"Which doctor did she go to?"

"I remember she said it was a Dr. Cameron in Strathbane."

Angela phoned the television studios in Glasgow and asked to speak to Elspeth Grant, saying she was a friend. She was told Miss Grant was broadcasting but if she left her name and number, Miss Grant would phone her back.

Worried that her husband might drop in, find out what she was doing, and accuse her of interfering, Angela paced nervously up and down. At last the phone rang and, with relief, she heard Elspeth's voice on the line.

"It's about Hamish," said Angela. "Have you heard he's to be married?"

"Yes, I got an invitation to the wedding."

"Elspeth, something is wrong. He is not happy. Josie is supposed to be pregnant. Could she be tricking him? Oh, Elspeth, I do wish you would come up here and find out for sure."

"Wait a minute. Are they living together?"

"No, Josie is at the manse with Mrs. Wellington. I assumed it was because people here are a bit old-fashioned."

"But he is seen out with her?"

"Yes, I saw them at the Italian restaurant just the other day. Hamish was quiet and polite. Josie chattered on and on. But there's more. Hamish went to my husband some time ago claiming he had been drugged and got samples and rushed off to the forensic lab in Strathbane with them. The lab said he was clear."

"I remember Lesley at the lab. She was keen on Hamish and I always think she upped and married her boss just to show him. Look, I'll get some leave of absence and get up there. But Hamish wouldn't fall for a fake pregnancy, if that's what it is. Doesn't she go to Dr. Brodie?"

"No, she goes to a Dr. Cameron in Strathbane."

"I'll see you as soon as I can."

Several times, Josie had been on the point of calling the whole thing off. She had hoped to get into bed with Hamish long before the wedding and therefore be able, possibly, to become genuinely pregnant. But Hamish had said that he would marry her and look after her, but he did not want to have sex with her. Josie had wept and pleaded but Hamish was adamant.

Her mother had arrived to stay at the manse. Flora McSween was thrilled to bits. Because Josie's father was dead, she was to be given away by her Uncle Bob. The wedding gown was a miracle of white satin and pearls.

Flora did not suspect anything wrong. Josie told her often how much in love she and Hamish were. Any odd bouts of weeping on her daughter's part, Flora put down to wedding nerves. She mostly lived in paperback romances and kept as much of the real world at bay as she could.

Hamish was loyal to Josie in that he did not confide in anyone how miserable he was at the prospect of being married to her. Never before had his police station home and his bachelor life looked so dear. There was only a trickle of work to keep him busy, although he travelled over his large beat as much as he could.

Strathbane, on the other hand, was in the grip of drug wars. Jimmy had agreed to be his best man but had not been near the police station and so had no inkling that Hamish was miserable at the prospect of the wedding. And for the villagers, Hamish put on a good front, smiling affectionately at Josie when they were out together, thanking people for their wedding presents, and saying, yes, he hoped the sun would shine on the important day.

*   *   *

Angela was feeling frantic. She had phoned Elspeth again, and Elspeth said that she was in difficulties trying to get away but would be there as soon as she could.

So it was a week before the wedding when Elspeth at last drove north and booked into the Tommel Castle Hotel. She dumped her bags in her room and went straight to the police station. There was no reply to her knock. She searched around until she found the spare key under the doormat and let herself in.

Elspeth studied the papers on his desk and found a map with a route marked in red. Hamish must be out on his beat. She picked up the map and decided to see if she could find him somewhere on the road. It would be better if she could ask him questions away from the village.

Hamish thought he would have felt less miserable if the weather had not been so glorious. Misery on a sunny day always seemed intensified. He had given up calling on people on his beat, feeling that he could not bear any more congratulations.

He parked on a hill above Braikie and tried to cheer himself up by thinking of the son or daughter he might have. But Josie had supplied him with warning pamphlets about how family pets could become jealous of a baby and about how they could cause dangerous allergies. He had shut her up by retorting that if that were the case, they would need to live separately.

Josie had handed in her notice. He stifled a groan. She would be there with him, night and day. How could he have been so stupid? He didn't usually drink much—only the odd glass of whisky—but he had drunk more than he usually did at that wedding.

They were going to Porto Vecchio in Corsica for their honeymoon. That was Josie's idea. Hamish had reluctantly agreed. Flora was paying for the wedding so he felt that he was obliged to pay for a honeymoon.

He got out of the Land Rover and let Sonsie and Lugs out as well. The mountains behind him soared up to a perfectly cloudless blue sky; in front of him the sea sparkled in the sunshine with myriad lights. The clean air smelled of thyme and peat smoke, wafting up from the chimneys of the town below him. Hamish gave a superstitious shiver. He suddenly felt as if he were seeing such a view for the last time.

A rifle bullet smacked into his chest. He caught a glimpse of Cora Baxter rising from the heather and hurrying off down the brae before he collapsed to the ground and blackness settled on him.

Elspeth drove through Braikie and out on the north road. Something off to her right caught her attention. She stopped and saw the police Land Rover up on the hill. She could just make out a uniformed figure lying beside it.

She ran up the hill, calling out, "Wake up, Hamish! It's me, Elspeth!"

But when she reached him and saw the dark stain of blood on his regulation jersey, she let out a wail of despair. Sonsie and Lugs were guarding the body. She took out her phone and shouted down it for help from the emergency services. Then she knelt down in the heather beside him, feeling for a pulse. There was one, but it was faint.

She pressed a handkerchief to the wound and whispered, "Oh, Hamish."

His eyes flickered open. He said in a whisper, "Cora Baxter," and then lapsed into unconsciousness again.

It seemed an age before she heard the whirring blades of a helicopter overhead and the siren of an ambulance coming out from the town.

The ambulance came bumping up the hill over the heather and the helicopter landed.

"He's been shot!" said Elspeth to the paramedics. "Cora Baxter did it."

"It's bad," said the leading paramedic. "The helicopter had better take him down to the Raigmore Hospital in Inverness."

"I'm going with him," said Elspeth. An oxygen mask was placed on Hamish's face. Elspeth climbed abroad the helicopter and sat beside Hamish, praying as she had never prayed before.

The news that Hamish Macbeth was in intensive care hit the village of Lochdubh like a bombshell. The whole village including Josie would have descended on Inverness had not Dr. Brodie informed them all that Hamish was not to be allowed any visitors.

Then further news came in that Cora Baxter had been arrested for the attempted murder of Hamish.

Josie fretted and worried. The wedding was postponed. If Hamish survived, he would expect her to be showing signs of pregnancy by the time he got out of hospital. She had been dieting so as to be slim on her wedding day. She decided the best thing would be to put on weight.

Because Elspeth had done such a dramatic piece on television, she was told to take as much time up in Inverness as she wanted. She was sitting in the waiting room when Jimmy Anderson arrived.

"What's the news?" he asked.

Tears rolled down Elspeth's cheeks. "It's still bad. They got the bullet out. He lost a lot of blood. But the bullet seems to have missed any vital organs and gone right through the shoulder. Why did that damn woman do such a thing?"

"These small towns," mourned Jimmy. "In a big city, to be a councillor's wife is no great shakes. But her position in the community had been everything to her. She must be mad. She knew what her husband had done and kept quiet about it."

The surgeon came into the waiting room and Elspeth jumped to her feet. "Any news?"

"He's stabilised but still unconscious. He should be coming out of it. I've seen something like this before but only with attempted suicides when they don't want to be rescued."

"I've got to talk to him," said Elspeth.

"I can't see it'll do any harm and it might do some good."

"Wait for me, Jimmy," said Elspeth. As they walked along the corridors towards Hamish's room, Elspeth whispered, "Don't tell anyone. But I think he has been conned into getting married. I've no proof. Just don't let his fiancée see him."

The surgeon was very impressed to be talking to such a famous Scottish celebrity.

"If he recovers, I'll see," he said.

Elspeth went into Hamish's room and sat down by the bed. "I'll give you ten minutes," said the surgeon.

Taking Hamish's hand in a firm clasp, Elspeth said, "It's me . . . Elspeth. Wake up, Hamish. What would Lochdubh do without you? Listen! Do you remember the time we went poaching up on the colonel's estate and caught that big salmon and the water bailiff nearly caught us? It was a grand day. How we laughed! And we poached that salmon for dinner. There are good times still to come."

Hamish lay as still as death.

"Oh, wake up, you silly cowardly bastard!" shouted Elspeth.

A doctor came hurrying in. "You are not to shout at the patient. I must ask you to leave."

"Elspeth," came a faint croak from the bed.

"Oh, Hamish," said Elspeth. "Welcome back."

The next day when Elspeth called again, it was to find Josie by the bed, holding Hamish's hand. The surgeon had felt he could hardly refuse Hamish's fiancée a visit.

"He's making a grand recovery," said Josie, "so the wedding will be going ahead quite soon."

"Are you sure, Hamish?" asked Elspeth.

"Of course," he said blandly. "Thank you for saving my life."

"I think Hamish and I would like some time together," said Josie.

Elspeth looked enquiringly at Hamish and he gave a brief nod.

Elspeth went back to the offices of the *Highland Times* in Lochdubh.

"Come back to work for us?" asked Matthew Campbell, the editor.

"No, I just wanted to borrow one of your computers and go through the local stories."

"Help yourself. Everything's on the computer now. All the cuttings are down in the basement."

Elspeth sat down at the computer, switched it on, and typed in "Dr. Cameron Strathbane."

No results.

Elspeth found a copy of the Highlands and Islands telephone directory and looked up Dr. Cameron. There was the name and address. She wrote the address down and set off for Strathbane.

The doctor's surgery was down near the docks in a far-from-salubrious neighbourhood. Even the seagulls looked dirty. Thin, white-faced youths lurked outside.

Elspeth had donned a simple disguise in the car: a woollen hat pulled down over her hair, glasses with clear lenses, and old clothes from her thrift-shop shopping days.

She sat in her car and wondered what to tell the doctor was wrong with her. Then she thought—but what good would it do? She took out her phone and called Jimmy, glad she had kept his mobile phone number form the old days when she used to work for the *Highland Times*.

"Elspeth!" said Jimmy. "What's the news about Hamish?"

"Recovering rapidly. Jimmy, have you heard anything about a Dr. Cameron in Strathbane?"

"Why?"

"Just passing the time up here looking for stories."

"I thought you grand presenters had reporters and researchers to do the work for you."

"Indulge me, Jimmy."

"It's last year's story. Cameron was up before the sheriff on a charge o' selling methadone to druggies. He got off because the laddie who shopped him disappeared."

"Thanks."

"But why . . . ?"

"I'll let you know if anything comes of it."

Elspeth thought hard. Before she tackled Cameron, she desperately wanted to know if the results of Hamish's urine test and blood test were accurate. They could still be in the forensic lab. But how to get them? If Lesley were alerted, she might destroy them.

She drove slowly to the forensic lab. Outside, she pulled off her glasses and hat.

Elspeth walked into the lab. Bruce and several of his assistants were working at long benches, strewn with not only the paraphernalia of forensic detection but also half-eaten sandwiches, flasks of coffee, and paperback books.

Bruce recognised her and rushed forward. "It's Elspeth Grant. What can we do for you?"

"I'm up here until Hamish gets better," said Elspeth. "I thought I might fill in the time by doing a feature on your lab. Have you time to show me around?"

"Sure. Care for a drink?"

"Not now."

Elspeth barely listened as he took her around the lab. At last she said, "And where do you keep the samples? The public have become very interested in cold-case files."

He led her into an adjoining room full of freezers. "All in here," he said.

"Goodness, you are efficient. Are they all labelled?"

Bruce gave her a superior smile. "Of course." He swung open one door. "See?"

Elspeth stared at the labelled samples. She could not see Hamish's name. "This is fascinating," she said. "May I see in the others?"

Bruce opened door after door. In one of them, in a corner, Elspeth saw two samples labelled HAMISH MACBETH.

They returned to the lab. "Where has everyone gone?" asked Elspeth.

"Lunch. Would you like to join me?"

"I'm a bit pushed for time but I wouldn't mind a drink. Whisky will do fine, if you have it."

He laughed. "This lab runs on it. Wait here. I've got a bottle somewhere."

When he went off to a side room, Elspeth darted back to the freezers, seized Hamish's samples, shoved them in her handbag, and hurried back to the lab.

Bruce came out holding a bottle and two glasses. "I thought

you'd have a cameraman with you," he said, pouring Elspeth a generous measure.

"I'll be back with one, but I just wanted to get a feel for the place first. Slainte!"

She knocked back her drink and said, "I've got to run. See you soon, Bruce."

Elspeth went to the nearest supermarket, bought a bag of ice, and put the samples in amongst the cubes. There was a forensic lab in Aberdeen. She could only hope they could get a result for her quickly.

But after a long drive to Aberdeen, she was disappointed to learn that the quickest they could do it would be two weeks. Still, she reflected, Hamish was safe for the moment. She decided to return to Glasgow.

Hamish, although still weak, was able to get out of bed and go for short walks. He pretended to be very frail, however, when Josie and her mother came to call, to hide from Flora his lack of affection for her daughter.

But just as he was pronounced fit to leave, Flora arrived on her own, very agitated. "Hamish, Josie has just told me she is pregnant and it's beginning to show. You must be married as quickly as possible."

Hamish looked at her wearily. It was all going to happen anyway. "Make it next week," he said.

Rapid invitations were sent out again with the new date. Angela stared at hers in dismay. She had been immersed in writing her latest book and had not been out and about to pick up the gossip or she would have heard of the new date before the invitation arrived in the post. Three days' time! She phoned Elspeth, who listened in horror to her news. In fact it was more like two days, as Angela had not opened her post until the evening.

"I'll do my best," said Elspeth. She knew she dared not ask for any time off, so she pretended to faint on the studio floor. The television doctor diagnosed overwork and stress. Elspeth left the studios and drove straight to the airport. She booked herself onto a flight to Aberdeen. At Aberdeen airport, she hired a car and drove to the forensic lab.

She was told they had not yet got around to examining her samples.

Elspeth took a deep breath. She faced the director of the lab and said, "Unless you get me these results fast, a man is going to be tricked into marriage."

"All right!" he said. "Come along tomorrow morning."

Elspeth booked into a hotel, barely sleeping that night, and was at the lab the first thing in the morning.

The director beamed and handed her a printed result. "This Hamish Macbeth had taken a big dose of Rohypnol. It's the first time we've had a man with this result. Macbeth . . . isn't that the . . ."

But he found he was talking to the empty air.

With the printout on the seat beside her, Elspeth drove the long way across country to Strathbane.

To her dismay, she found that the surgery would not open

until six o'clock in the evening. She tried to find the doctor's home address but without success.

Impatiently she waited and then, just before six, she donned her disguise. A thin, undernourished-looking girl was just unlocking the door to the surgery when she walked across the road and followed the girl in.

"Are you the receptionist?" she asked.

"Yes."

"I need an urgent appointment."

"Doctor has people to see before you."

Elspeth slid a twenty-pound note over the desk. "I need to see him quickly."

The girl tucked the note into her blouse. "Take a seat. He won't be long."

The surgery began to fill up with young men and women, all shabby, all with dilated pupils. He's still up to his tricks, thought Elspeth. I'll nail the bastard, but Hamish comes first.

Dr. Cameron arrived, a small, rotund man with a fat face and little gold-rimmed spectacles. The receptionist followed him into his office and then came out again after a few minutes. She jerked her head at Elspeth. "You can go in now."

Elspeth switched a powerful little tape recorder on, leaving her handbag open, and went in.

"Now, then," said Dr. Cameron. "What's all the rush?"

"I want to get married," said Elspeth.

He grinned. "Can't help you there."

"As a matter of fact, you can. You can do for me what you did for my friend Josie McSween. You gave her a certificate to say she was pregnant when she wasn't pregnant at all. You didn't even examine her. Josie gave me your name."

Careful not to disturb the tape recorder, Elspeth pulled five hundred pounds out of her handbag and put them on the desk. "Will that do?" she asked.

He counted out the notes. "Josie McSween gave me one thousand pounds," he said. "That was the deal."

Glad she had drawn out a large sum of money earlier, Elspeth took out her wallet and counted out another five hundred.

Again he checked the money. He drew his prescription pad forward. "Name?"

"Heather Dunne."

"Address?"

"Number six, the Waterfront, Cnothan."

He scribbled busily and handed the note over.

"Nice to do business with you, Miss Dunne. Don't come back."

Elspeth drove to the centre of town and sat in her car. She hated Josie with an all-consuming rage. She could go straight to the police station and hand the evidence to Hamish. But she wanted Josie to suffer as much as Hamish had suffered. She wanted her to be publicly humiliated.

Josie was at the manse, trying on her new wedding gown, altered to fit her larger figure.

"Why did you have to go and put on weight," fussed Flora,

and then flushed nervously as she remembered in time that no one was supposed to know that Josie was pregnant.

"I think she looks a picture," said Mrs. Wellington, her eyes full of sentimental tears.

All Josie wanted was to get the dress off, get rid of everyone and sneak out into the garden where she had hidden a bottle of vodka. She was suffering from nerves. When she wasn't drinking, the enormity of the way she had tricked Hamish would hit her. But with drink inside her, all her rosy dreams of domestic life with a loving Hamish came back to her, giving her courage.

Her friend Charlotte and husband Bill were staying at the manse. Charlotte came into the room, wearing a maternity gown, just as Josie was being helped out of her wedding dress.

"Oh, put it on again, Josie. I must have a look."

Clasping her hands into fists to hide their shaking, Josie struggled back into the gown with the help of her mother.

"You look a picture," breathed Charlotte. "Do you remember the last time I saw you, Josie? I'd just discovered I was pregnant. And do you know, it was the strangest thing. After you'd left, I searched and searched for that pregnancy kit and I couldn't find it anywhere."

Flora, who had bent down to check the hem of her daughter's gown, suddenly felt a qualm of unease. Would Josie? Could Josie? No, banish the very thought.

"Come on, Hamish," said Jimmy, "have a dram."

The kitchen was full of men. Hamish had refused to hold

a stag party so the male villagers had all crowded into the police station instead.

"I want to have a clear head," protested Hamish. He forced a smile. "It's not every day I get married. Oh, just the one, then."

How Hamish bore that evening, he did not know. Everyone got very drunk. Angus, the seer, had produced a pair of bagpipes and begun to play. He was not a good player and the horrendous noise filled the kitchen. The flap on the kitchen floor banged as Hamish's pets fled from the noise. Hamish heard them go. He was worried about them. They had picked up on his distress, and when they saw Josie, the cat would hiss menacingly and the dog would growl.

At last they all left with the exception of Jimmy, who was to be best man. Hamish helped him into the bed in the one cell and then sat down at the kitchen table and stared bleakly into space. The flap banged and Sonsie and Lugs came in. The dog put a paw on Hamish's knee and stared up at him with his odd blue eyes.

"What's to become of all of us?" said Hamish.

Josie sat in her room, drinking from the bottle of vodka she had collected from the garden.

As the liquor burned its comforting way down, her hands stopped shaking and the rosy dreams came back. Everything was going to be all right.

Angela desperately tried again and again to call Elspeth. But she was not at the television studio and she had her mobile switched off. She wondered whether to go and see Mrs. Wellington. But what proof did she have? And everyone in the village was very excited about the wedding.

She went to the church—which was never locked—sat down in a pew, and prayed that somehow, something would happen to stop the wedding.

Chapter Twelve

☠

Behold while she before the altar stands
Hearing the holy priest that to her speaks
And blesseth her with his two happy hands

—Edmund Spenser

The day of Josie's wedding to Hamish Macbeth dawned bright and sunny. The village buzzed with anticipation. Those who were not married found the whole idea of a wedding romantic, and those who were had a feeling of schadenfreude that some other poor soul was about to be chained in holy matrimony.

Cottage bedrooms reeked of mothballs as rarely used finery was taken out to be put on. Men grumbled that their suits had shrunk and the more tactful wives refrained from pointing out that they had put on weight.

The Currie sisters, each donning a large hat, looked like a couple of small toadstools, for the hats were of brown straw topping their camel-hair coats.

Josie squeezed herself into a body stocking and took a swig

of vodka to stop her hands shaking. Her mother came into her room to help her put on the wedding gown.

"Your face is all blotchy!" exclaimed Flora. "You smell bad. Have you had a bath?"

An excess of vodka sometimes does not smell like alcohol but more like a nasty body odour.

"It's just nerves," said Josie, spraying her armpits with deodorant. "Help me on with my dress and then I'll make up my face."

In the police station, Hamish stood before the wardrobe mirror in his bedroom, dressed in a rented morning suit, and surveyed himself miserably in the glass.

Jimmy came in, similarly attired. "Cheer up, Hamish. It's your wedding day. And you're going off on your honeymoon. Think of all that hot sun."

If only I could win the lottery, thought Hamish. We could live in separate houses. Why on earth did I not just promise to pay maintenance for the child and remain single? But in his heart he knew that in an old-fashioned village like Lochdubh it would be looked on as a scandal. Daviot would never stand for it. Seducing a policewoman!

"I gather we don't have a limo to take us to the kirk," said Jimmy.

"It's only a few yards. We walk."

"Your ma must be pleased."

"Aye, she's looking forward to seeing some grandchildren," said Hamish. He had been avoiding his family of late, frightened that that strange highland telepathy might pick up on his distress. He had not even introduced Josie to them, making excuses time after time that she was out on a job.

"Well, let's go," said Jimmy impatiently. "Want a drink?"

"No." Hamish made his way to the kitchen door. He bent down and patted Lugs and Sonsie. Angela had promised to look after them while he was on honeymoon.

They walked out of the police station and on to the waterfront. It was a perfect day. Hardly a ripple disturbed the blue waters of the loch. A group of fishermen heading for the church gave a ragged cheer.

Hamish looked around himself bleakly. He felt he was saying goodbye to all the happy times he had known. "Man, you're as white as a sheet," said Jimmy.

The church was full to the bursting point. He took his place at the altar with Jimmy at his side and sent one last desperate prayer upwards. "Dear God, if there is a God, get me out of this!"

"You look right miserable," hissed Jimmy.

"I'm still a bit weak," said Hamish. Priscilla Halburton-Smythe had sent him a congratulatory message from Australia along with her apologies that she was unable to attend.

There was a murmur of anticipation. Then the choir burst into a rendering of "You'll Never Walk Alone." "Yuk," murmured Jimmy. "Did you think o' that one, Hamish?"

"Nothing to do wi' me," he muttered.

Then Charlotte, Josie's bridesmaid, hurried up the aisle and said to Hamish, "You've got to come outside. Those wretched pets of yours are stopping Josie entering the church. It's a disgrace, that's what it is."

Hamish ran down the aisle and outside. Josie stood there on the arm of her uncle. In front of them, barring the way, stood Sonsie, hissing, fur raised, and Lugs barking like mad.

"That's enough!" shouted Hamish. "Off home the pair o' ye."

They slunk off and Hamish went back into the church and up to his former position at the altar. The choir, which had fallen silent, burst out into song again.

Hamish stared straight ahead as Josie made her way up the aisle.

Jimmy turned round. "My, she's got fat," he said. "Has she got a bun in the oven?"

"Shut up!" said Hamish.

When Josie stood next to him, he stared straight ahead.

Something's far wrong here, thought Jimmy suddenly. He's hating this. What can I do now? I can pretend to have lost the ring. Maybe that'll help.

Hamish did not listen to the opening words of the marriage service.

Then Mr. Wellington said the piece about anyone having any reason against this marriage to speak now or forever hold their peace.

The church doors crashed open and a clear voice said, "I have."

There was a babble of shocked alarm as Elspeth strode up the aisle.

"Explain yourself," shouted Mrs. Wellington.

Elspeth faced the congregation. "This woman, Josie McSween," she said, her voice dripping with contempt, "has tried to trick Hamish into marriage. At one time, I believe, she doped his drink with Rohypnol—it's commonly known as a date-rape drug. She pretended she was pregnant. Hamish took a urine sample and a blood sample to the forensic lab in Strathbane. They lied to him and told him he was in the clear. I have confirmation from a forensic lab in Aberdeen."

Her eyes ranged over the congregation and settled on Lesley and Bruce. "Yes, I took the samples out of your lab. So sue me! Josie got a certificate from a shady doctor in Strathbane to say she was pregnant. I wondered whether he would admit to it. Listen to this!"

She switched on the tape recorder. The congregation listened in appalled silence. Josie turned to flee. Charlotte shouted after her, "You stole my pregnancy kit, you wee bitch!"

Flora hurried after her daughter. Josie jumped in the limousine, waiting outside. Her mother climbed in after her.

"Perth!" shrieked Josie to the driver as the congregation began to stream out of the church.

Lesley and Bruce found Daviot looming over them. "You are suspended from duty pending a full enquiry," he said. "Not another word."

As they went off, Daviot turned round and saw Jimmy. "Where is Hamish? This is awful. I am sure he is not recovered from that shooting."

"He's down on the beach," called Angela.

They all rushed to the waterfront wall.

Hamish Macbeth was turning cartwheels along the beach with the dog and cat prancing beside him.

Instead of being delighted that Hamish had escaped being tricked into marriage, a good number of the villagers were feeling positively sulky. They trooped up to the manse to retrieve their wedding presents. They thought that at least the reception might have gone ahead and let them enjoy a party, but Flora had stopped on the road to cancel everything. Because Flora had employed a catering firm who were already packing everything up, there was nothing they could do but mutter that Hamish should have known something was wrong.

In the police station later, Jimmy said the same thing. "Had ye gone daft?" he asked. "Couldn't you tell when you'd had sex or not?"

"How could I think otherwise?" said Hamish. "I woke up and there she was, in the bed. Then she gets proof she's pregnant. What else could I do?"

Superintendent Daviot walked into the kitchen without knocking. "This is a bad business," he said. "I want a full statement from you, Macbeth. Forensic experts are hard to find. There's to be a full enquiry. Josie McSween is not fit for the police force. She will need to make a statement as well. But I cannot understand how an experienced policeman like yourself came to be tricked."

Hamish was beginning to wonder the same thing himself but Jimmy leapt to his defence.

"How was he to know, sir?" he asked. "A good copper goes by the evidence, and Josie had all the evidence."

"Dr. Cameron has been arrested," said Daviot. "He won't weasel out of this charge the way he did the last one."

"How did Josie get the Rohypnol?" wondered Hamish. "Maybe she got it out of the evidence room. There was a case last year where it was used."

"The press are all gathered outside," said Daviot. "You'll need to speak to them or we'll never get rid of them."

"Could you do that?" asked Hamish. "You're awfy good wi' the press."

"I will do that now," said Daviot, who adored getting any sort of publicity. "We'll put it out that you are still weak after that shooting. Where were you supposed to be going on honeymoon?"

"Corsica. Tomorrow morning. For a week."

"Then I suggest you take yourself off there while we sort things out here and return in time for the board of enquiry."

Daviot left the kitchen and soon his voice could be heard outside, making a statement.

"Where's Elspeth?" asked Hamish. "I owe her a lot."

"She's up at the hotel."

"Tell Daviot I've gone for a walk to clear my head."

Hamish slid out of the kitchen door followed by Lugs and Sonsie and started the long walk by way of the fields at the back to the Tommel Castle Hotel.

He was directed to Elspeth's room and knocked at the door. When she opened it, he said, "How can I ever thank you!"

"Come in, Hamish, and bring the beasties with you."

Hamish sat down wearily. "Thon was one great piece o' detective work, Elspeth."

"You need to thank Angela as well. She was worried about you. I guessed because she told me you'd gone to Dr. Brodie for blood and urine tests that you were sure you'd been drugged. Then there's Josie. Angela was sure you didn't care anything for her. I just wanted to make sure."

"You'd make a better seer than auld Angus any day. He didn't suspect a thing. Look, Elspeth, this is short notice but I've got plane tickets to Corsica and the hotel is booked—single rooms, mind. I've been told to take a break. Why don't you come with me?"

"Maybe I could. I've been told to take some leave."

"I'll get Josie's air ticket changed to your name. It'll be great to get away. The press'll be hounding me for a week. We'll need to be at the Inverness airport at six in the morning."

Elspeth was suddenly very happy. "We can make it."

"Right. I'll just use your phone and see to that ticket."

Josie and her mother were sitting gloomily in a hotel outside Perth. As the limousine had turned into their street, Flora saw press ranged outside their house and told the driver to reverse quickly. She had left Josie in the hotel and had gone back to pack up clothes for them to wear, not wanting to return to Lochdubh. The press followed her when she left after loading two suitcases into the limo. "Can you lose them?" she asked the driver frantically.

"Sure," he said. By shooting two red lights in Perth, racing up the A-9 at one hundred miles an hour, and then swerving off the road and up a farm track, he was able to hide out until the pursuers roared past.

Flora had been left very comfortably off but she felt bitterly that Josie's caper was costing her a fortune as she paid off the driver and tipped him handsomely. Then there were gratuities paid to the staff of the hotel so that they would deny ever having seen them.

"It's all Hamish's fault," said Josie. "I'd have made him a good wife."

"You're mad!" said her mother, and Josie burst into tears.

The police called for her two days later and told her a police car was waiting for her downstairs to take her to Strathbane. The hotel staff were willing to lie to the press but not to the police. Flora wanted to go with her but was told firmly to stay behind.

"I'm going home, Josie," she said as Josie was led from the hotel. "If the press are there when you get back, you'll just need to face them."

Angela said to her husband, "Hamish has gone off to Corsica with Elspeth. Do you think they'll get married?"

"God forbid. This village has had enough of Hamish Macbeth and his weddings. And the sooner he gets back here and picks up those pets of his, the happier I'll be. That cat of his frightens me to death."

Josie, on her way into police headquarters, was stopped by Blair. "Tell them that Macbeth led ye on," he said. "Tell them he wound ye up."

So Josie, dressed neatly in a tailored suit and white blouse with her hair brushed and shining, said in a low voice that she was so very sorry, that Hamish had wooed her and led her on.

But because she had proved herself to be an expert liar, this was not believed—which she saw immediately from the stony faces looking at her. The interview went on for a long time as they dragged everything out of her, from taking the date-rape drug from the evidence room, to drugging Hamish, to faking evidence that she was pregnant.

Finally, Josie was told to wait outside. She sat miserably on a hard chair in the corridor. She felt numb.

When she was called in after ten minutes, she was told she was no longer welcome on the police force. Hamish Macbeth had phoned from the Inverness airport to say he would not be pressing charges. They wanted the whole scandal hushed up as quickly as possible. If Josie talked to the press, however, they would press charges against her.

Downstairs, nobody looked at her as she made her way out. She now had to drive to the manse in Lochdubh to collect her clothes. She had begged her mother to do it for her, but Flora had hardened towards her daughter and told her to do it herself.

She hoped against hope that Mrs. Wellington would be out when she arrived, but that lady was in the kitchen. "I'm sorry," said Josie.

Mrs. Wellington was stirring something vigorously on the stove. She did not turn round. "Get your things and go," she said.

When she had everything packed up, she took her suitcases out to the car and drove out of Lochdubh. As she was approaching the Tommel Castle Hotel, she suddenly thought that one drink for the road would brace her. She went into the bar and ordered a whisky.

Mr. Johnson came in after she had sat down with her drink and began talking to the barman. She went up to him. "Is Miss Grant staying here?"

"No she's not," he snapped. "She's gone off to Corsica with Hamish."

Josie slowly sat down again. How could they do this to her? It was *her* honeymoon.

Hamish and Elspeth spent a few blissful days either walking around the old walled Genoese town of Porto Vecchio or swimming at the beach of Palombaggia, a dream of white sand and clear blue water protected by pink granite rocks. Hamish said he still felt a bit shaky, and in the evenings, he liked to sit in some café or other watching the people go by.

Elspeth talked about her work at the television station. Unlike Hamish, she felt she could not relax because she knew there were a good few women who coveted her job. At times, when Hamish was dreamily sitting looking out at the crowd, she had an impulse to rush to the airport and get the next plane home. It was not as if Hamish showed any romantic feelings towards her. He treated her more like a male friend and at night they both retired to their separate rooms.

On their fourth evening there, Hamish suddenly said, "If you got married, would you leave your job?"

"No," said Elspeth. "Well, maybe. I haven't had much success with men."

Hamish was wondering whether to propose. He did not relish the idea of moving to Glasgow. Elspeth was easy and affectionate with him. She could always work for Strathbane Television. Horrible although the experience with Josie had been, it had put the idea of children into his mind. A son or daughter would be great. He had seen jewellers with pretty rings. He had been on the verge of proposing to her for so long but something had always thwarted him. Perhaps it would be a good idea just to take the plunge and see what they could work out.

Back in his room that evening, he thought that perhaps he would find out if there was any news of Priscilla. He obscurely felt it would be some sort of way of saying goodbye to the love that had plagued him for so long.

Elspeth was sitting out on the balcony of her room when she clearly heard him telephoning and asking for news of Priscilla. Always Priscilla, she thought. She went indoors, determined not to hear any more.

Over breakfast the next morning, Elspeth noticed that Hamish was glowing with happiness and excitement. "I think I'll take myself off for a look at the shops this morning," said Hamish. "Don't bother coming with me."

"I'll probably stay here on the terrace and read," said Elspeth. She was suddenly determined to follow him. She felt he was up to something.

Hamish stopped in front of a jewellers' window. Then he went inside the shop. The door was open. Elspeth heard him saying, "I'm looking for an engagement ring."

So that was that, thought Elspeth. That phone call and then all his happiness and excitement at breakfast. Priscilla must have arrived back from Australia and he must have proposed to her on the phone. And he didn't say a word to me!

I have risked my career for that bastard, she thought, as she returned to her room and hurriedly packed. I am not even going to leave a note for him. I just want out of here.

When Hamish returned to the hotel, he went straight up to Elspeth's room. There was no reply to his knock. He decided to go down onto the hotel terrace and wait for her.

After an hour, he went in to the desk and asked if Miss Grant had left a message for him.

He was told to his horror that Miss Grant had checked out. He took a taxi to the airport. He was just in time to see Elspeth disappearing through Departures.

"Elspeth!" he shouted. But she did not turn round. He tried to get through into Departures but was told he could not pass. He begged and pleaded. He said he was a police officer, but to no avail.

What had gone wrong? If she had been called back to Glasgow, why had she not left a note for him?

But as he wearily returned to the hotel, he began to feel very stupid indeed. He had kissed her good night on the cheek but, apart from that, he had not shown any romantic feelings towards her. Perhaps she had felt she had done enough for him and had got bored.

By evening, though, a strange thing had happened. With Elspeth gone, he could not remember what had prompted him to want to propose. When she was with him, he felt their companionship was so strong that surely he was in love with her. But if he were in love, he should be feeling heartbroken. He decided to treat himself to a lobster dinner that evening and forget about the whole sorry business.

Flora was seriously worried. Josie was hardly ever sober. At last, she confronted her daughter. "Josie, either you go to an AA meeting or I'm turning you out."

"You wouldn't," gasped Josie.

"I would that. Here's the address. Get yourself along there this evening. You haven't started drinking yet today and you're not going to. I'm going to watch you like a hawk every minute."

Flora drove Josie to a church hall that evening and said grimly, "I'll be back to pick you up when the meeting is over."

Josie walked into the hall. All the faces seemed like a blur. She sat down at a large table. The meeting began. The secretary said, "As usual at this meeting, we go round the room and introduce ourselves."

When it reached Josie, she clasped her shaking hands and said, "My name is Josie, and I am an alcoholic." And with that, she burst into tears. The man seated next to her put an arm around her shoulders. "You'll be all right," he said, handing her a clean handkerchief.

Josie barely listened to the speaker. The man next to her had his hands on the table. She could see his sleeve and an edge of white shirt with cuff links. He was wearing a gold watch. Josie dried her eyes and stole a look at his face. It was a square handsome face, and he had blue eyes.

At the end of the meeting, she said, "Can you help me?"

"We could go for a coffee, if you like," he said.

"Oh, my mother will be waiting outside to take me home."

"It's important you get help," he said. "We'll tell her I'll drive you home."

Josie's mind rocketed into romance immediately. He looked rich. He was miles better looking than stupid Hamish Macbeth. Life was definitely looking up.

And there was that bottle of vodka she had hidden in the garden, just waiting for her.

Epilogue

O Caledonia! Stern and wild!
Land of brown heath and shaggy wood,
Land of the mountain and the flood,
Land of my sires! What mortal hand
Can e'er untie the filial band
That knits me to thy rugged strand.

—Sir Walter Scott

Lochdubh settled back into its usually lazy life as a rare fine summer spread across the Highlands of Scotland.

Hamish appreciated his life as never before. Any crimes he had to deal with were small. He covered his extensive beat, glorying in the landscape. He had only two worries. Elspeth had not returned any of his calls. And he had not been demoted, so there was still the threat of another police officer being billeted on him.

As autumn came around, he travelled down to the High Court in Edinburgh for the trial of Jamie Baxter. He endured a long cross-examination by the defence stoically. By the time it was all over and Jamie was sentenced to three life terms for the three murders, he felt tired and edgy. Elspeth came back into his mind. Glasgow was only a short distance away. He decided to call on her and see if he could find out why she had left Corsica so abruptly.

But at the television studios, the receptionist, after phoning to see whether Elspeth was available, said sweetly that he would need to leave his name and number and Miss Grant would get in touch with him—if she wished.

He knew where Elspeth lived so he drove to her flat down by the River Clyde, parked, and waited. It was a long wait but policemen were used to long waits on doorsteps.

At last at ten in the evening, he saw her drive up the street and park. She got out of the car. She looked slim and elegant, not at all like the frizzy-haired, thrift-shop-dressed Elspeth he had first met when she was a reporter on the *Highland Times*.

A red sunset was setting over the waters of the Clyde. Little fiery points danced on the choppy water as he climbed down from the police Land Rover feeling stiff and awkward.

"Elspeth!"

She swung round at the entrance to the flats and stared at him. "What is it, Hamish?"

"What iss it, lassie? You ran away from me in Corsica, you didn't answer my calls, what on earth did I do?"

"Nothing."

"Then *why*?"

"Hamish, I'm tired. Do we need to go into this now? All I want to do is get to bed."

"Yes, now. Can we go inside?"

"No. Look, Hamish," lied Elspeth, "I phoned the studio that evening in Corsica and they said someone was trying to take my job. I panicked. I didn't stop to think. I just rushed off to the airport."

"But you met me for breakfast the following morning and you didn't say a word!"

"Look, I left on an impulse. I'm sorry, okay? Now if you don't mind . . ."

She turned away from him and went into the block of flats.

Hamish climbed slowly back into the Land Rover and sat deep in thought. What on earth could he have done? That evening before she left, had he said anything to put her off? He remembered that phone call to the hotel and how he'd asked for news of Priscilla. Could she have heard him? Then he remembered that the windows to his balcony had been open; and if Elspeth's had been open; well, she could have heard him. What if she had followed him in the morning and heard him asking for an engagement ring and assumed it was for Priscilla? Was that it?

Oh, what's the use, he thought. Just let me get back to Lochdubh.

Elspeth stood at the window. She suddenly turned and ran out of her flat and down the stairs to the street. But she was just in time to see the Land Rover turning the corner and disappearing.

*   *   *

Josie McSween was married. She was now Mrs. Jeffries, married to a divorced lawyer she had met at a meeting, the one who had given her his handkerchief. They had been married quietly in a registry office and had gone to Paris on honeymoon. But even in Paris there were bloody AA meetings where she sat moodily glaring at slogans with legends like LIVE AND LET GOD and wondering what God had ever done for her.

Still, a lot of sex had counteracted her cravings for drink until they were back in Perth and Tom Jeffries, her husband, was once more immersed in work. She knew she did not dare even have one drink because as Tom had pointed out, you can't bullshit the bullshitters and he would know the minute she had lapsed.

For fear of the press, the wedding had been kept very quiet. She longed to show Hamish Macbeth and all those creeps in Lochdubh that she was now a rich, married lady.

So one Saturday, she startled her husband by proposing that they drive up to Lochdubh. "I know I had an awful time there," said Josie. "But Sutherland is very beautiful. We could just drive along the waterfront at Lochdubh but not stop."

Tom had been so busy since the honeymoon that he felt he had been neglecting her. He was disappointed that Josie did not seem to have made any friends amongst the women at the Perth meeting. But, he thought, it was early days. It took some people quite a long time to settle in.

Josie relaxed in Tom's BMW and looked out the window as the car smoothly moved over the humpbacked bridge and on to the waterfront.

But to her horror, there was the tall figure of Hamish Macbeth, standing in the middle of the road, holding up his hand. Tom slid to a stop and lowered his window. "What's up?" he asked.

"There's a great big hole in the road ahead. You'll need to turn round. Why, Josie? Is that you?"

"Yes," muttered Josie.

Tom looked at the tall policeman in surprise. "Are you Hamish Macbeth?"

"Yes, I am."

"Josie and I are married."

"Congratulations," said Hamish.

Tom made a three-point turn and drove off. So that was Hamish Macbeth. Josie had described him as quite old and with a sour face and little eyes. But the Hamish he had just met had been an attractive-looking man with fiery red hair and clear hazel eyes. He felt a pang of unease as he glanced at his sulky wife.

"Let's just go home," said Josie.

How she endured the rest of the weekend until Tom went back to work, Josie did not know. Every fibre in her body was screaming for a drink. Just one, she thought. Just one little drink.

When Tom went to work on Monday morning, Josie headed for the supermarket. She wandered down the aisle amongst the wines and liquors in a trance.

In his office, Tom phoned his AA sponsor. "I'm worried about Josie," he said.